"George Carlisle hired me to kill you."

Daria stared wide-eyed at Detective Kevin Gordon, the man who'd just uttered the most frightening words she'd ever heard.

George was trying to kill her?

Daria nervously shook her head. "You must be mistaken. George is a lot of things—I don't have enough fingers on both hands to count them—but he's not a murderer."

"Exactly. This is why he sought out someone else to do his dirty work."

She turned to the hard sound of his voice. "Is George in jail?"

Kevin paused. "No."

"Why not?"

"We arrested him last night. But we didn't have enough evidence to keep him."

"If you can't put him in jail, why are you here? Why are you even telling me all this?"

Kevin drew in a deep breath. "Because I need you to understand. If you stay in town, you're going to die."

Books by Lisa Mondello

Love Inspired Suspense

Cradle of Secrets
Her Only Protector
Yuletide Protector

LISA MONDELLO

Lisa's love of writing romance started early when she penned her first romance novel (a full fifty-eight pages long, but who's counting) at the age of ten. She then went on to write a mystery script that impressed her sixth-grade teacher so much he let her and her friends present it as a play to the whole grade. There was no stopping her after that! After going to college for Sound Recording Technology and managing a Boston rock band for four years, she settled down with her husband of over eighteen years and raised a family. Although she's held many jobs through the years, ranging from working with musicians and selling kitchen and catering tools, to teaching first- and second-graders with special needs how to read and write, her love of writing has always stayed in the forefront, and she is now a full-time freelance writer. In many ways writing for Steeple Hill Books feels like coming home. Lisa lives in Western Massachusetts with her husband, four children (who never cease to amaze her as they grow), a very pampered beagle and a rag doll cat who thinks she owns them all.

YULETIDE PROTECTOR

LISA MONDELLO

Steeple
Hill®

Published by Steeple Hill Books™

STEEPLE HILL BOOKS

Steeple
Hill®

Recycling programs
for this product may
not exist in your area.

ISBN-13: 978-0-373-44368-0

YULETIDE PROTECTOR

Copyright © 2009 by Lisa Mondello

www.SteepleHill.com

Printed in U.S.A.

Jesus said unto him, If thou canst believe, all things are possible to him that believeth.
—*Mark* 9:23

This book is dedicated to the men and women in law enforcement who protect and serve.

A special thank you to Officer Tom Naujoks and Officer Dave Mellen who listened to my wild ideas patiently and helped me plot and research this story. Any mistakes in interpreting facts are my own.

ONE

The six-foot-high chain-link gate was locked tight. Kevin Gordon tested it, curling his fingers around the metal, and gave a quick yank.

It didn't budge. He knew it wouldn't. The owners had long since packed up their lunch boxes and paperwork, washed their hands of grease and filth and headed home.

George Carlisle, the man he'd agreed to meet here, was only using this salvage yard on Water Street for their meeting. It looked empty enough. But it was always better to be safe than to be dead.

Satisfied, Kevin carefully moved down the cracked sidewalk, sidestepping a concave square that rainwater had gouged out. A quick glance down to the intersection told him the streets and the crossroad were barren, with no movement except from scraps of newspaper and discarded wrappers that caught the wind and rolled across the asphalt.

No respectable citizen would be caught dead walking these Providence streets at this late hour of the evening. But George Carlisle wasn't exactly respectable and neither was the meeting he had planned. At the moment, though, it was just Kevin and a menacing junkyard dog testing the fence with every jump as Kevin walked along the sidewalk.

"Easy, boy," he said quietly, which only aggravated the dog further. The Christmas lights that had been strung across the top of the fence blinked colors of red, white and green, making the dog's snarl look even more threatening when the colorful light hit its face. Deciding the location was as secure as it was going to get, Kevin focused on his backup. Pulling the hood of his gray winter jacket over his head to conceal his earpiece, the undercover detective said, "You with me in the van, Jake?"

"Reading you loud and clear, Kev." He recognized his partner, Jake Santos, as the man speaking into his ear. "There's no one moving around out here."

"Ski, anything moving from where you're sitting?" The only things moving where Amery Stanasloski was perched were his fingers, Kevin figured. A hint of a smile played on his lips. The kid, fresh out of police academy, was probably sitting on his hands right now either to keep them warm from the winter chill or to just still them. Amery had the eyes of an eagle, but a nervous habit of tapping his fingers. Sitting on the rooftop of the foundry building on the corner, Ski had a bird's-eye view of the blocks below him. Yeah, Kevin could just picture the kid perched high on a wooden crate like a hawk on a cliff.

"That's a negative here. And you're coming through loud and clear," Ski said, but Kevin could barely hear him as the receiver was filled with so much static that Kevin's hand instinctively went to his ear.

"Do you hear that static in the van, Jake?"

"You're both clean here. Must be on your end."

Irritation coiled inside Kevin. A half hour ago when

he had tested it, the earpiece was working fine. Now it was too late to go back to the van and get a backup.

"I'm ditching the piece."

Jake's voice came over the radio, his voice firm and hard. "Keep it, Kev."

"I'm liable to blow this whole meeting if I get feedback and flinch. What if Carlisle can hear it? I'm ditching the piece."

"That's a neg—"

Kevin yanked the earpiece out of his ear and dropped it deep into his jacket pocket.

The connection to the team was critical, but the most important factor was making sure the meeting went off without a hitch. Even without audio communication, Kevin knew that Ski was in position to make sure that if anything turned sour, he'd be at Kevin's back in half a heartbeat to take Carlisle down. He'd be fine, even without the earpiece.

As he moved, Kevin said a silent prayer to the Lord, as he did every time he went on duty. *The Lord is my helper, and I will not fear what man shall do unto me.* Normally he and Jake said it together, but without his earpiece, their connection was gone. Still, Kevin knew his partner's faith in the Lord to guide them on these streets was as strong as his.

The sound of a twig snapping had Kevin turning his attention to the dark figure hanging in the shadows on the sidewalk by the corner of the junkyard. The Doberman snarled on the other side of the fence and would no doubt continue until they'd moved on.

The man stopped moving, to Kevin's dismay. It wasn't a good idea for them to meet in the shadows where the team didn't have a crystal-clear view of what was going on. A quick flick of a switchblade or the draw of a gun could end it all for one of them in a matter of seconds.

"You waiting for the morning light?" the man said, his voice low and scarcely audible above the rustle of unfurled leaves moving with the late-evening winter wind.

"I didn't think you'd show," Kevin said, intentionally keeping his voice lower in an effort to draw the man closer to him. It didn't work.

His pulse pounded, and the muscles in his stomach squeezed tighter. Kevin moved a few feet forward and into the shadow, ignoring the snarling dog following his movement.

He cut to the chase. "Are you Carlisle?"

"You expecting someone else this time of the night?" the man asked with heavy sarcasm.

Without a name, some definitive proof, this meeting would be a bust. Kevin pushed harder. "Answer the question. I like to know who I'm talking to."

"Yeah, I'm George Carlisle. Satisfied?"

Kevin could hardly see Carlisle's face in the darkness. The shape of his nose, the square of his jaw looked like the pictures Ski had taken less than a week ago. But in this blackness, it was hard to be sure.

"Word is you're in need of a service."

Carlisle nodded. "That's right."

Kevin forced the words out of his mouth. *Make him talk. Get it all on tape.* "What do you want?"

"I want you to kill my ex-wife."

He'd known it was coming, but Carlisle's words still had Kevin's blood running cold. He played along. "Just tell me how you want it and I'll get it done."

"It needs to be soon."

"I don't like being rushed."

Carlisle's voice turned hard. "It's my dime."

Cold disdain froze Kevin's insides. "I can accommodate you if the price is right."

"And…make it quick. Bottom line. There should be no trace back to me."

"You don't want any last words? Some final message?"

"Just kill her."

Kevin's jaw clenched. "Her" would be Daria Carlisle. At one time, she had probably loved the man who was now arranging her death. How could any man conceive such a horrible plan?

A low-hanging tree limb concealed the glow of the distant streetlight, casting a long shadow like a finger stretching toward him, as if in warning.

"How do you want it done?"

Carlisle laughed and that sent a chill worse than the night air straight up Kevin's spine. "If you have to ask, maybe I've come to the wrong place."

"That's your call. But there isn't anyone better than me to do the job and you know it," Kevin said tightly. "This is business and I like to be clear about what I've been hired to do. There's no room for misunderstandings and I don't like mistakes."

"I've heard that about you."

The rumor that Kevin was a high-priced assassin had reached Carlisle's ears, just as he'd hoped it would. As much as meetings like this disgusted him, his job as an undercover cop filled Kevin with pride. By playing his part, he'd be able to get George Carlisle put away where he couldn't hurt his ex-wife ever again.

For the first time, Kevin realized Carlisle wasn't looking at him at all. He was looking around, checking shadows and the empty streets, paying no mind to the Doberman who was still barking out his objection to their presence.

Carlisle stopped searching the street, but still didn't look Kevin directly in the face. "Her name is Daria Carlisle. She lives alone in some run-down house on a side street by the highway. And I want you to kill her. I don't care how. I just want you to do it quick."

It was all Kevin could do to keep from reaching out and grabbing this monster by the throat. Dragging in a steady breath, he focused on what he had to do.

He didn't want to think about how close Daria Carlisle had come to ending up in a cold grave. If Carlisle had approached anyone else, she probably would have. His chest hurt just thinking about it.

Kevin was here for Daria Carlisle, even if she didn't know of the danger she was in. Tomorrow she'd know the truth and by the time he told her just what her ex-husband had planned to do, she'd already be safe.

Backup was in position and ready to haul this beast away as soon as Kevin gave the signal. He'd be the one to slam the cell door on George where he'd most likely spend the next twenty years to life. He was never going to hurt Daria Carlisle.

"Mr. Carlisle. I think you and I can do business."

And for the first time that night, Kevin smiled.

"George Carlisle hired me to kill you."

Daria stared wide-eyed at Detective Kevin Gordon, the man who'd just uttered the most frightening words she'd ever heard.

"Excuse me?" she muttered.

He spoke the words again as she stood almost glued

to her kitchen's aged linoleum floor. She hadn't really needed him to repeat himself. She'd heard the words perfectly fine the first time. But even after the second round, the words hadn't sunk in.

George was trying to kill her?

She'd woken so happy that morning, intent on starting the day by rummaging through the Sunday paper for a used miter saw. She needed one to finish off the woodwork in the one-hundred-and-fifty-year-old house she'd purchased because she'd fallen in love with the backyard.

Her gaze swept from the strong lines of the detective's face to the floor as she dragged in a breath of air. Earlier that day she'd been obsessing over how she was going to afford replacing the linoleum, especially with Christmas shopping just around the corner. In the span of moments, her priorities had shifted drastically.

The coffeemaker stopped burping behind her as the pot reached full capacity, and the sudden silence reminded her to breathe. She'd forgotten she'd been making coffee for both of them.

When Kevin had approached her at the holiday gift market, showing her his badge and asking her to come to the police station so they could talk about something serious, the last thing she'd wanted was to spend her Sunday stuck inside what was probably a smelly old building. So she'd spontaneously invited the nice detective home with her for coffee. She'd foolishly thought he wanted to question her about the vandalism that had been happening in the neighborhood, and what better way than to show him the graffiti spray painted on the side of her house.

She'd had no idea the serious talk was about her ex-husband.

Daria cleared her throat and gazed uncertainly at the tall man who was now occupying a seat at her kitchen table.

"Did you hear what I said?" he asked.

She nodded, trying to steady her trembling hand. "Yes, I did."

He sighed. "I know you're probably a little shocked right now. We can still go to the police station to discuss this if it'll make it easier."

He stayed seated, clearly doing his best not to crowd her as he filled the space between the table and the wall.

Daria tried not to think about how before he'd introduced himself as a detective and flashed his badge, she'd actually found herself so utterly attracted to this man with the dark blond hair. She still was.

"I don't know how you can make hearing your ex-husband has hired a hit man to kill you any easier."

"True. Maybe you should sit down, Mrs. Carlisle. You're not looking well."

As Kevin stood, he dragged the ladder-back chair out from beneath him until it hit the patched wall. The caustic sound of wood being dragged over cracked linoleum made Daria jump, but she remained rooted in place.

Her eyes focused for a fleeting moment on the tattered wall where the chair connected with ugly, old wallpaper she hadn't yet gotten around to stripping. She'd been patching and repairing this barely inhabitable old house since shortly after filing for divorce. Unlike this house, her marriage had not been fixable.

"I know you're scared. And I'm sorry. I wish there was an easier way to tell you. Would you like me to call a friend to come over? You really shouldn't be alone."

"I'm not alone. You're here."

And unfortunately, there was no one to call. No one

she'd want to confide in about something like this, anyway. She'd only been living in the house for six months, and hadn't gotten to know her neighbors. And most of the time when she wasn't working at her job at the bank, she was working on home repairs and hadn't really had a chance to make friends.

"After the night I had battling with the captain and district attorney, I could sure use that cup of coffee. Why don't you take a load off while we discuss what's happening with your ex."

She didn't really want to talk about George anymore. It had been a difficult decision to file for divorce from George, but it had been her decision alone. And from that moment on George was no longer her husband, no longer her present or future. He was only her past. And she was determined to leave the past behind her.

"My divorce from George became final just about eight months ago. I never see him anymore."

Kevin nodded and sighed.

"And you really are with the police?" she asked.

Blue eyes glanced at her with amusement. "You've never seen a police badge before, have you?"

"It's not a habit I have, no. For all I know, the badge you showed me in the market is something out of a gumball machine."

He gave her a tired grin. "Don't worry. A lot of people get fooled, but I assure you I'm a police officer. You can call the station and check if you want. In fact, it's probably a good idea to get in the habit of doing that. You never know who you're dealing with."

A hot rush of blood flamed her cheeks as the events of the morning began to play in her mind. "So this wasn't really a chance meeting we had this morning at the market?"

He shook his head. "After I finished up at the station this morning, I stopped by here and found your truck in the driveway, but you weren't home. I'd seen you at the market a few weeks ago picking up the Sunday paper, so I figured maybe it was something you did every Sunday morning after church. I was right."

Half-right, but she didn't bother to correct him. The only time she'd ever been in church was for a funeral of someone she knew. Her wedding had been at City Hall. Her parents had never rejected faith, but they didn't embrace it, either, and it was something that had never been a part of Daria's life.

"I didn't realize anyone was following me."

"Keeping tabs from a distance. You weren't supposed to notice and you didn't."

Someone had been "keeping tabs" on her, watching her move through her daily life, and she'd had no idea. A chill raced up Daria's spine, making her shudder.

"You say you met with George last night?"

"That's right."

"Was that your first meeting?"

"For me, yes. Before that, I'd only seen him from a distance."

Daria leaned against the counter and nervously pushed her fingers through her hair. "If my life is in danger, why am I just hearing about this now? Why didn't anyone come to me sooner?"

"Until last night, there was only suspicion, no proof. I couldn't very well come to you with suspicion of a possible conspiracy to murder you until I knew for sure that was George's intention. Just because someone says they want to kill their spouse doesn't mean they'll actually do it or hire someone else to do it. A lot of people say things in the heat of the moment. Most times it never comes to a meeting and it ends there once people blow off steam."

"But George contacted you?"

"We had the word of an informant that George Carlisle was hunting for a hit man to kill his ex-wife. Things moved to a new level last night when I finally met with your ex-husband and he made his intentions clear. Your life really is in danger."

Kevin sat back down at the table. It was then that she noticed the fatigue pulling at his crystal-blue eyes. He had nice eyes, darker blue on the outer edges to define the clear blue of the center. They were warm, with a spark of life that blazed when he laughed. She'd noticed them right away when she'd seen him at the market. How could he have been following her without her spotting him?

Daria nervously shook her head. Deep inside she felt like crying, but no tears would come. "You must be mistaken. George is a lot of things—I don't have enough fingers on both hands to count them—but he's not a murderer."

"Exactly. This is why he sought out someone else to do his dirty work. He gets what he wants without getting any blood on his hands."

Those words weighed heavy on her mind as Daria poured black coffee into a pair of coffee mugs. She suddenly felt the need to talk to her mother and father. To have some connection with someone safe. But her parents were still in Mexico and didn't have a phone in their villa.

"Why would George want me dead? We haven't seen

each other in months. What possible reason would he have after all this time?"

"He may have been planning it since before the divorce."

She turned to the hard sound of his voice. "Is George in jail?"

Kevin paused. "No."

"Why not?"

"We arrested him last night. But his attorney had him released this morning because we don't have enough evidence to keep him."

Her hands were shaking when she put the coffeepot back on the coffeemaker's burner. Cream. Had Kevin said he wanted some? She put some on the table in front of him along with a spoon.

"I don't understand any of this," she said quietly. "You just said he contacted you last night. Isn't that proof enough?"

"I'm afraid not."

"Why not?"

The lines on Kevin's face seemed to deepen. "I messed up."

"Excuse me?"

To his credit, Kevin didn't even try to look away like most people did when they were feeling guilty. Instead, he looked straight at her. "I was fitted with a wire. But somehow the signal got scrambled. None of the words George spoke to me during our meeting were recorded. There was nothing at all but static. But since I'd taken out my earpiece, I didn't realize my team couldn't hear what was going on. And thanks to the shadows we were standing in, they couldn't see us clearly, either. George made a move toward me—he was reaching out to shake my hand, seal the deal—but another officer thought I was being attacked and moved in to arrest George. My cover was blown. And without any hard-core evidence or corroborating witnesses to my testimony, the D.A. won't prosecute him. She won't even touch the case."

Ignoring his coffee, he leaned forward, resting his elbows on the table.

"I take full responsibility. The officer who made the arrest is a first-year cop and I should have anticipated him being eager to move in. I didn't know the detectives in the van couldn't hear what was being said or I would have aborted the meeting long before Officer Stanasloski moved in."

"So George just goes free? Just like that?"

"Unfortunately, yes. For now." Kevin swallowed hard, then looked directly at her. "We're still watching him. Although, it'll be harder now that he knows there is police involvement and we're onto him."

"Terrific," she said with a heavy sigh.

"Look, I know you're scared and I don't blame you. No one wants to hear that their life is in danger, especially from someone they cared about. Thing is, men like George don't stop. He'll keep going. Now that my cover is blown, he'll find someone else to take my place. And he'll be more careful next time. No matter how much you want to believe there isn't a threat to your life, I'm here to make you see the truth."

Daria shook her head. It was all too much. "There has to be a mistake. You must have misunderstood what he said. I can't imagine George being that vicious. He's not that kind of man. Even when we had our biggest fight—when I filed for divorce—he never lifted a hand against me."

"Desperate people do desperate things, Mrs. Carlisle."

"If you can't put him in jail, why are you here? Why are you even telling me all this?"

Kevin drew in a deep breath, stretching his shirt taut against a wall of muscles that were his chest and shoulders. "Because if you stay in town, you're going to die."

TWO

"I suggest you leave Providence as soon as possible. As in, right now," he said.

It was hard to find her voice behind the mammoth-size lump of fear clogging her throat. He'd said from the start that George had tried to hire him to kill her...but somehow hearing the words—that she'd die if she stayed in town—made it all feel very real. "You're not making any sense at all."

Shrugging, he said, "I know and I apologize. It was a long night. But if you'll listen to me for a minute, you'll understand that it's the only way to ensure your safety."

Kevin stood up and yanked the chair next to him away from the table, motioning with his hand for her to sit.

"Please."

Her glance darted from the chair to his angular features. "To be perfectly honest, I'm not sure I want to hear any more of this."

Blue eyes that seemed much too sincere for what they were discussing penetrated her. "I'm afraid that's not an option. But we do have a crisis counselor at the station. If you want, we can go—"

"No! I don't want to go to the police station." Somehow going there now would make all of this worse.

Daria's chest hurt. Weighing the burning fear she felt against the simple act of sitting next to this man she'd been so attracted to at the market, she decided she was being utterly foolish. He was only speaking words.

Sticks and stones may break my bones but names will never hurt me. The taunting childhood song echoed in her head. Didn't that apply to words, too? There was nothing Detective Kevin Gordon could say that would hurt her.

She did as she was told, seating herself at the table and folding her hands in front of her. Never in her life had she felt so shaken.

She couldn't believe it. George kill her? No. It wasn't possible. The man who'd wooed her with white roses and cried when he'd asked her to marry him? The man who would have given her anything she asked for?

Not that she ever did, Daria thought with a pang of regret. It was one of the differences between them that ultimately destroyed their marriage.

Daria blinked away the sudden tears stinging her eyes and forced memories of their marriage from her mind. Back then she'd always wanted to please George and always seemed to come up short. But that was in the past. She wasn't letting anyone else make decisions for her now.

Abruptly, she got up from the table and strode out of the kitchen, down the hall and into her bedroom. She quickly threw open the double doors of her closet and rummaged through the shelf until she found the hatbox where she kept her special keepsakes. Clutching the box to her chest, she brought it into the kitchen and plopped it down on the table in front of Kevin.

"What's this?"

"Pictures. I don't have many. I didn't feel the need to keep them, but…"

She paused when she found the picture she'd been searching for, the only photo of the two of them she'd taken with her when she'd left George. She stared at it for a long time, trying to imagine George actually doing what Kevin said he'd done. She handed it to Kevin.

"This is my ex-husband with me on our wedding day."

Kevin stared at the image, his square jaw tight, his posture straight as he scrutinized the faces of two people who'd been so happy that day.

"Is this the man you met with last night? The man who said he wanted you to kill me?"

She held her breath as he continued to stare. She had to know for sure. Couldn't Kevin be talking about someone else? It had to be someone different. Anything else was unthinkable.

"He looks different," he said sharply as he tossed the photo in the box.

Relief washed over her whole body, leaving her trembling and weak. She let out all her breath in one quick burst. "Then there has been a mistake."

"No, I'm afraid not. Your ex-husband looks different in this picture than the ones we have on file. His hair is lighter now, thinner. But I'm afraid it is the same man I met with last night at the salvage yard."

The relief Daria had felt just a few short seconds ago now vanished, leaving her cold.

"Would it really matter if it wasn't George?" he asked. "There'd still be someone out there who wanted you dead. Your life would still be in danger."

Would it have mattered? Yes, Daria realized. Some

crazy stranger with a blank face trying to kill an unsuspecting woman was a lot easier to take than knowing someone she used to love wanted her dead.

"Look, George probably seemed like a great guy when you were with him. But even seemingly nice guys can be dangerous."

Kevin ran his hand down his face, rubbing his shadowed jaw for a few seconds. "I know you want to believe that this isn't happening to you. I wish it weren't. It must seem like a nightmare," he said delicately.

He had no idea.

Tears sprang to Daria's eyes and she clamped her teeth over her bottom lip when it started trembling. She shoved the picture back into the hatbox and slammed the cover on top.

Kevin sat back down at the table, brought the mug of coffee to his lips to take a sip and then dropped it on the table again. His grimace only magnified his fatigue, deepening the creases carved around his crystal eyes.

Daria automatically picked up his mug, brought it to the sink and dumped it out before pouring a fresh cup.

"What are you doing? You didn't need to do that," he said, his eyes wide with surprise.

"You didn't like it."

She was trying too hard to please again, Daria realized. It was a bad habit she'd gotten into with George. She'd let him dictate her life, make all the decisions, because it had been important to him to have a submissive, obedient wife. She wasn't that woman anymore. But the habit was hard to break.

"It's okay," Kevin said. "I usually load my coffee with sugar. I'm more inclined to get my caffeine from the soda machine than the coffeepot at the station because their coffee can be pretty nasty."

"I'm sorry. I don't have any sugar," she said quietly as she placed the fresh cup of coffee in front of him.

"It doesn't matter."

"I don't have any soda either, I'm afraid." She flipped a lock of hair behind her ear, feeling the same sense of panic hit her square in the chest.

"Stop apologizing." Then his voice softened. "You didn't do anything wrong. This isn't your fault."

Daria held up her hand. "You were there. Can't you testify against him?"

"Sure. But all we have is my word against his. That's sometimes enough to make an arrest but not enough to make it stick. We need the audio file for it to stand up in court. Since George has a high-priced lawyer and no ironclad proof against him, we had no choice but to let him go. As soon as he hit the street, I came over here to warn you."

She fiddled with a paper napkin, wiping a stubborn dried ring on the table.

"We tried to say that he was acting out of character by even being on the scene, but George's doorman backed his statement that he goes for a walk nearly every evening. The doorman verified that George left at roughly the same time he usually does when he takes his walk. Even got concerned when George didn't return as usual. George was at the station at that point."

"George suffers from insomnia," Daria said, staring into the coffee she'd poured for herself, but hadn't sipped. The wrinkled napkin lay beside her cup, wound as tight as a toothpick. "Taking a walk helps him sleep."

"That's what he said."

Daria closed her eyes for a brief moment. "So what are my options? Do I get police protection? An escort? Guard dog or something?"

"No."

"No? I don't get any help from the police at all?"

Kevin sighed. "We've set it up so that your street will be patrolled more often. But we just don't have the resources to offer protection custody except for witnesses that are set to go to trial."

"So, you'd be able to protect me if I actually saw my ex-husband commit a crime, but since he didn't kill me and I can't testify you can't do anything?"

His mouth twitched. "That pretty much sums it up."

She stared at him in disbelief for a moment. "Well, I guess that's that then. Thank you for stopping by, Detective. I appreciate the warning. If you hear of anything else, please be sure to let me know."

Kevin stared at her, his eyes wide with confusion. "Mrs. Carlisle, you do understand everything I've just told you, don't you?"

Anger surging through her, she balled her fists in her lap. "Please don't call me that anymore. I'm not Mrs. Carlisle. My name is Daria."

"Okay, Daria. You can't stay here. As I said earlier, you need to leave as soon as possible."

Uncurling her fingers, she planted her palms on the table, pushing herself out of her chair. She grabbed her full coffee mug and dumped the contents into the sink along with the mug, watching the liquid slosh up the sides and splash the faucet with the force of her movement. Her eyes stung with the hot tears she was holding back.

Leave here? Was he kidding? Her whole life she was

leading up to the very thing she'd finally achieved when she'd bought this house. She finally had a home. After nearly twenty-six years of living out of boxes with her vagabond family and making new friends every few months, only to have to leave them, *she* finally had a chance to dig in some roots and call someplace home.

Standing at the sink, she stared out the kitchen window to her backyard. Right now the ground was cold, but in a few months it would be bursting in green with the coming of spring. But even in winter it looked beautiful to Daria because she knew this place had all the makings of something wonderful. Something that would be *hers*.

And he wanted her to up and leave? Where would she go? She couldn't afford to go to Mexico to stay with her parents. And she certainly couldn't afford to buy or rent someplace else to live in. It had taken every penny she still had after the divorce to buy this place. She had no savings left. There wasn't a friend from her past she could call that she felt close enough to impose on, either.

Kevin's deep voice floated to her and broke into her thoughts. "You can leave here. The sooner the better. Go someplace far away and set up in another town someplace. Change your name, even. We have it within our resources to help you do that. You can make it so that it seems as if Daria Carlisle really is dead. Or at the very least, fallen off the face of the earth. Do whatever you can do so that George Carlisle and whoever he may hire in the future won't have a chance to find you. If you stay here, you aren't safe."

She spun around to look him in the face. There was no teasing there, no slight twitch of his lips to indicate Kevin was about to burst into laughter as he told her the punch line of his joke. There was no punch line, she realized.

"No."

"Excuse me?"

"You heard me."

"I don't think you understand. The police can't protect you. Leaving is the only way."

"I'll get a dog. A big one."

"A dog isn't going to do squat against an assassin's bullet."

Her back straightened. "Okay, then I'll hire a bodyguard." With what, she didn't know. Hiring a bodyguard meant spending a great deal of money and she was already mortgaged up to her eyeballs. "I mean, how long would I have to be watched anyway? It's not going to be forever, right?"

His incredulous laugh came out in a short burst. "I can't believe this. You're actually considering staying here? I have no idea how long you'll need protection. And hiring a bodyguard that really has the ability to protect you would cost far more than just leaving."

Kevin looked at her as if she had five heads. She sounded insane. Of course she did. But how could he know what this house meant to her? What it represented?

"Well," she said, "I'm staying. You see, I just bought this house a few months ago. I know it doesn't look like much now, but I'm going to be spending the next week stripping layers and layers of cruddy wallpaper in my bathroom so I can see just how awful the walls are in there and decide whether or not I have enough money to retile or just spackle, paint and stencil. And if I have enough money, I want to buy a big Christmas tree for my front window. I don't care that I don't have a lot of ornaments to put on it. I want to be in my own home for Christmas. My home. Not some hotel somewhere or someone else's house. The only relocating I want to be doing is moving junk from this house. And I'm not included in that."

Kevin pulled himself to his feet, towering over her. He had to be well over six feet tall, dwarfing her average height.

He poked his finger on the table. "You don't understand how serious this threat is."

She charged back. "Oh, yes, I do. But you're telling me I have to just up and leave my house, the home I've spent the last six months pulling apart to make livable again. Do you have any idea what this house looked like when I moved in?"

He started to speak, but she halted him by raising both hands in the air.

"It was awful. Truly hideous. I had a small fridge and microwave in my bedroom up until a month ago. I had to be careful where I stepped for fear the stairs would break, and there are still places I have to watch out for when I'm upstairs. I had to buy a membership to the gym just so I could shower there until I'd saved enough money to pay for new plumbing, which, let me tell you, costs a pretty penny in an old place like this."

She stalked to the back door and swung it open, letting in a rush of cold air that blew her hair into her eyes. She swiped the errant strands away with a quick brush of her hand.

"Do you see that tree out there?"

Kevin leaned forward to peer out in the direction she was pointing.

"The little one that looks like a twig being held up by a stake?"

She huffed. "It's a hummingbird vine. I planted one

of these with my mother when I was ten years old when we lived in Georgia. We'd only stayed there for about five months. I remember I was so excited about watching something that I had planted grow and bloom. Why? Because I never have. I never stay in any place long enough to see it."

She also recalled her mother's comforting pat on the back when Daria asked if they'd be there in the spring to see it bloom and the disappointment she'd felt when her mother said no, that they were planting the tree for someone else to enjoy. That was the story of her life. Digging roots for someone else.

Daria took a deep breath, afraid her voice would crack if she spoke too soon. "I know you don't get it. But I've never seen the same bush shed its leaves and then bloom the next summer. I've never lived anywhere long enough to see more than two or three seasons change."

She swung the door shut and stared at Kevin.

"I planted over three hundred dollars' worth of bulbs this past fall. Even when the rest of the house was still too decrepit to live in, when I couldn't stand to nail one more board inside, I still came out into the yard and dug in the dirt because I couldn't wait to see what my garden would look like next spring. I knew without a doubt that this time I'd be around to see it bloom."

Kevin interrupted before she could continue. "You're clearly upset. But you can't compare a garden to your safety."

"I've spent my entire life living out of boxes, never unpacking because there wasn't any point unpacking. We never stayed anyplace long enough for it to matter. This is it. This house. The end of the line for me."

She felt the tears spring to life in her eyes. No one else could understand what this house meant to her.

"I'm not going anywhere. Not George, my parents or even the Providence Police Department is going to make me leave the only home I've ever had in my life. This is the place where I plan to spend the rest of my life until the day I die."

Kevin stared at her hard, her shoulders sagging under silent resignation. "If you stay here, it may be sooner than you think."

Kevin paused for a moment before saying more. He should have insisted Daria come to the station. Maybe there he could get her to see sense. He wasn't getting through to her here. He knew she'd be upset. How could she not be? And he took responsibility for that. If he'd done his job properly, she wouldn't be in danger.

He should never have taken the earpiece out. If he hadn't, he'd have known the wire was somehow compromised. He would have played out last night differently. He could have let George walk away. It would have killed him to let the man go after what he'd heard him say about Daria, but he wouldn't have blown his cover. George wouldn't know the police were aware of his intentions to hire someone to kill his ex-wife.

What he should have done was play along and wait until money had changed hands. Then he could have arrested him. Nothing George Carlisle did after that would keep him a free man.

But high on the rooftop, Ski hadn't been aware nothing was being recorded, either. He'd moved in too quickly. And the entire sting had been compromised.

All night, he'd replayed everything he'd done

wrong. And now Kevin was faced with a woman who would risk her life just to stay in a house! It reminded him of those people who waited too late to leave the area around a volcanic mountain even when they knew it was about to explode.

He had to make her understand that leaving was the only way to keep her safe from her ex-husband.

"You can't compare your life to a few flowers in the garden. You can always get another house somewhere else."

"That's easy for you to say. You're not the one being asked to give up everything."

He scrubbed both hands over his face, the long night and his own emotions dragging him down. "Your ex is not going to stop."

"He knows the police are onto him now. Are you going to keep watching him?"

"As much as we can. But he'll just be more careful who he associates with."

She stared out into her backyard through the kitchen window, the sunlight highlighting her strawberry-blond hair and wide blue eyes. Her tense, drawn expression was quite a contrast to the bright smile he'd seen when he'd spoken to her at the market.

He'd noticed her smile first, and immediately recalled her ex-husband's words and the twisted look on his face. And he'd been thinking how insane it was for anyone to want this beautiful woman with such a sunshine smile dead.

"Don't be naive. It's only a matter of time before George contacts someone else, offers big money to do the job."

"How much did he offer you?"

"Fifty thousand," he said as delicately as possible.

She started laughing and covered her face with both hands. "Now I know he must have been joking. A sick joke, but still a joke."

He felt the crease between his brows. "Why?"

"George doesn't have that kind of money. I can't even figure out how he could pay a 'high-priced' lawyer."

Kevin blew out a breath of frustration. "Daria, do you know what kind of dealings your ex-husband has?"

She gave him a slightly frosty glance. "Of course I do. His dealings are what eventually led to our divorce."

"Then you're aware that in the past he has taken out very high-interest loans with some disreputable people?"

"George likes to spend money. He never has any, but he likes to spend it. And yes, I'm aware he did business with loan sharks in the past. He has a habit of living beyond his means."

"Other than the loan sharks, where did he get the extra money?"

"I don't know."

Her voice had a tinge of bitterness to it. He glanced around her home and realized the divorce had done more than change her address. If she had been used to living in high style, she'd changed fast.

"But you knew of his dealings?"

"Not completely." She tapped a finger on the table and just stared out at nothing. "We were married while I was still in college. After I graduated and got a good job, we decided to save for a house. Or rather, I saved. He spent. His work as a broker makes good money. I didn't think it would take us long to save enough for a down payment. Unfortunately, no matter how much money George made, he never got quite enough money to satisfy himself. There were times I wondered where his extra money was coming from, but he'd tell me it was a bonus or something at work."

"And you believed him?"

Daria walked to the sink, grabbed a sponge and ran it under water, squeezing it before wiping the spilled coffee on the counter. With every stroke she wondered how she could have ever been so wrong about a person.

"I was young. I didn't know what to believe. I never saw his paycheck—I just knew he seemed to always be buying things or spending. But he came home one night, his face as white as a sheet, and told me he needed a lot of money. He said if he didn't pay it back fast he'd end up crushed like a tin can."

"So you gave him the money you had saved for your house."

She laughed sarcastically. "What else was I supposed to do? He said he'd made a mistake and convinced me he'd never do it again. I loved him…or at least I loved the person I thought he was. Sometimes you make foolish choices when you're young. Apparently, I was more foolish than I thought." She frowned, seeming lost in thought for a moment, then returned her attention to Kevin.

"Look, I really do appreciate you coming by here this morning and…filling me in on what's been going on. I'll be sure to be more careful to watch for anyone following me. Maybe this time I'll even spot you."

Her attempt at a joke fell flat.

"If you're not leaving, you leave me no choice but to continue watching you."

"I'm not leaving. Besides, I know George. You probably shook him up good. I'm not letting anyone drive me from my home."

* * *

Daria had spent her whole life trying to please her parents, trying to please her husband. She'd promised herself this time that she'd stand firm and not let anyone get in the way of her pleasing herself.

It had been a huge step for her to buy this house on Hitchcock Street. She'd wanted a real home for as long as she could remember. She could barely afford it and she was always strapped for cash to do repairs, but it was hers. It was home. And it was all she had. She couldn't leave even if she wanted to. Everything she had was wrapped up in this house.

Folding her arms across her chest, she said, "I think I need a little time alone." She had to do some thinking. Make her own decision about what to do next without any outside interference.

"There's no way I can change your mind?"

"Right now, no," she said resolutely, squaring her shoulders.

Kevin sighed, his shoulders sagging. "Then you leave me no choice. If you don't leave, then neither can I."

"What do you mean?"

"I'm your new bodyguard."

THREE

"You're still here?"

Kevin had parked his SUV against the curb right at the bottom of her driveway. His car was running and the frost that had formed overnight was now melted off.

He'd been sitting in front of her house all night. Daria knew this because she'd spent the better part of the night alternating between questioning her decision to stay in her house, running financial numbers on her calculator and peeking out the window to see if Kevin's SUV was still there. It was.

"Don't you have a job to go to?" she asked.

"I will, as soon as I know you're in your office building."

Daria glanced behind her toward the sound of the barking dog. Her next-door neighbor's Labrador, Spot, was at it again. No doubt garbage would be all over the sidewalk by the time she got home and Mrs. Hildebrand would have a few choice words to say in blaming her for the mess.

Turning to Kevin, she said, "My neighbors are going to think it's you that's stalking me. Not my ex-husband."

"No, they won't. I've met them already. I didn't want

them to be frightened when they saw my car sitting out at the curb all night, so I went over and introduced myself."

Daria's mouth dropped open. "You did?"

He pointed to the houses across the street. "Mrs. Parsons is thrilled to have an officer in the neighborhood. She said there've been a lot of hoodlums vandalizing their property for the last couple of years. Her fence has been knocked down twice in the last three months."

"Mrs. Parsons?"

Kevin threw her a suspicious look. "Don't you know your neighbors?"

"I just moved in."

"You said you moved in six months ago. What have you been waiting for?"

A fingernail of irritation crawled up her spine. "I've been a little busy trying to fix this house up so I can move my microwave out of my bedroom. I didn't have time to go door to door. You know, my neighbors haven't exactly sent out a welcome committee, either."

Daria glanced back again toward the sound of the dog. "Have you met Hilda yet?"

Kevin glanced at the house directly next to hers. "You mean Mrs. Hildebrand?"

Daria nodded.

"Hers was the first door I knocked on. Said your house used to be quite the party hangout for the local kids when it was empty. Hence the graffiti on your siding. She's a real nice lady. She grew up in that house, you know. She inherited it when her parents died. She baked me peanut-butter cookies, too. Want one?" he said with a lift of his eyebrows.

Daria peered into the truck at the half-full plate of cookies. "No."

"Suit yourself. They're really good."

Peanut-butter cookies? Daria couldn't believe it. "You mean she was actually nice to you? You had a real conversation?"

"Yeah, she's a sweetheart."

Daria's mouth dropped open. "She yells at me every single morning for putting my trash can too close to the property line and then blames me when the trash somehow ends up on her property. She'll never admit it's her own dog making the mess. Not that she's ever seen it. She's as blind as a bat."

"That much I figured out when she answered the door and thought I was her brother Edgar. She told me all about the vandalism here. It's only been in the past few years. Probably some street kids with nothing better to do. Despite the problems here, you picked a good neighborhood to buy in."

"Then you can understand why it would be hard to leave."

Kevin hesitated. "I can understand someone like Mrs. Hildebrand wanting to stay. She doesn't know anything else. But you just got here. You don't have any ties to this neighborhood like Mrs. Hildebrand, or Mrs. Parsons, who's been here for fifteen years."

"You got awfully chatty with my neighbors."

"I'm a police officer. People skills are important. So what's your reason for wanting to stay so badly that you'd risk your life? I know it's not bulbs in the backyard or nice crown molding in the living room. You can get that anywhere."

"You wouldn't understand."

He opened his SUV door and climbed out, leaning his full weight against the side of his truck. "Try me."

Daria stared into Kevin's face as he waited, with interest in his eyes. He had beautiful eyes, she had to admit.

"My parents moved around when I was growing up. A lot. My last count was that I've lived in over thirty-five different places. I stopped counting when I got married. Although the moving didn't end there. George always wanted a bigger place. Something more luxurious."

"Were your parents in the military?"

Folding her arms across her chest, she said, "No, my dad is an artist." She shrugged with a smile and glanced down the narrow city street as a car pulled out of the driveway. Someone else on their way to work. "They were typical children of the sixties who never quite moved beyond that era. Of course, you'd never know it to look at them now. But they still go on their occasional marches and still believe their one voice will save the world and make it a better place."

And unlike Daria, they believed that staying in one place too long would steal her father's creativity and make him stagnant. Daria believed it would keep her grounded. She was just beginning to feel that way here until Kevin had dropped his bomb about George.

"You see, when I bought this house I promised myself it would be the end of the line for me. I figured the only way I'd be leaving here is in a body bag."

Bad joke. She knew it the moment she'd uttered the words. The dark cloud that shadowed Kevin's face just proved it.

"That's precisely what I'm trying to avoid," he said in a voice that was much too deep and ominous to keep her from shuddering.

She cleared her throat. "Look. I know you don't understand. Unless you've lived the way I have, you never will. You won't see why this house is so important to me. Or why I can't leave."

"It's just a house, Daria." His words sounded so cold, although she was sure he hadn't meant to be harsh.

Tears stung her eyes. She knew it was impossible for him to comprehend how she felt. He'd probably lived in the same house his whole life just like Mrs. Hildebrand.

Daria pushed up the sleeve of her winter coat and glanced at her watch. She had to get to work. "Are you going to follow me all the way to the office?"

"That's the plan. As soon as I know for sure you've made it into your building I'll head out."

"When do you get to sleep?"

"I slept a little bit in the car last night. And when it got too cold I went for a walk and checked out the yard to make sure no one was lurking."

"I heard Spot barking."

"He's a good watchdog. If anyone had been loitering around here, Spot would have barked and I would have been on top of it. It's kind of nice having a dog in the neighborhood."

"Yeah, real swell. Maybe I should get one, too."

Daria sighed. Spot was a sweet dog and even though he always managed to make a mess in her yard, she liked him. It was Mrs. Hildebrand's bark Daria hated being on the receiving end of.

"I need to go," she said.

Kevin smiled, fatigue pulling at the corners of his eyes just like the morning they'd met.

"What time will you be coming home?"

She tossed him a wry grin. "I thought you said you were keeping tabs on me."

"I know your routine. In to work at nine, out the door

at five-thirty every evening. I'm asking just in case you're planning to run errands after work."

"If you insist on this insane idea of watching over me, I should be home a little before six."

Kevin watched as Daria turned her back and walked to her truck. He was struck by how odd it seemed to see a woman so elegantly attired in a dress coat, skirt and heels climb into that old clunker. She didn't seem the type to drive an old beat-up truck. For that matter, she didn't seem the type to be living alone, fixing up this old house, either. But then, what did he really know about Daria Carlisle...other than that she was stubborn?

Kevin turned the key in the ignition and heard the engine roar to life. He would watch her walk into her office building and then he would drive away. Her building had security and for now that was going to have to be enough. Besides, Ski was watching George Carlisle. But covering all the bases didn't take any of the edge off his fear that a guard in her building was not enough.

Daria was one stubborn woman. She was trading her life in exchange for watching a tree bloom next year. And she'd called him insane?

No, she'd called the idea of him watching over her insane. Well, Kevin couldn't really argue about that.

Shaking his head as his foot hit the gas pedal, he wondered just how long he'd be able to keep this up.

At the red light, he pulled in behind Daria's truck and watched as she glanced into her rearview mirror and caught him staring back at her. He didn't look away. He wanted her to know that he was serious. He was watching. He'd have his eyes on her until he was absolutely sure she was safe from George Carlisle.

Maybe after a few nights of him staring at her front door, watching her stare back at him from her bedroom window, she'd get the point and leave town as he'd suggested. Otherwise, he was going to have to get used to sleeping in his car for however long it took until they got enough evidence against her ex to put him behind bars.

Daria's office was a twenty-five-minute ride from her house. Kevin had clocked it, as well as the time it would take him to get from the station to her house. There was lag time. It couldn't be helped and it worried him greatly, but there wasn't a whole lot he could do about it.

He watched her gracefully step out of her truck and waltz into her building, never looking back at him. Stubborn woman.

When she was finally out of sight, he realized he felt no relief. Not for her. Not for him. Agitation crawled beneath his skin.

The woman didn't want to believe she was in danger. The district attorney and his superiors didn't want to put forth the resources to ensure her safety. And Kevin was only one man. He couldn't do it all.

Lord, please keep Daria in Your watchful eye when my own eyes can't be there to guard over her. Keep her safe from harm. Keep those who are trying to hurt her at a distance.

When he was finished with his prayer, he sighed. He had just enough time to get to his apartment, shower and change and then get to work. After the long night he'd had, he knew this day would be even longer.

The flowers were sitting in the center of her desk when Daria had arrived in her office. The excited stare from her administrative assistant was telling, but nothing was said. Yet. It was only a matter of time before Marla burst.

Daria hung her coat and stuffed her purse in the bottom drawer of her desk, locking it. Instead of the normal local radio station playing on a nearby radio, Christmas carols floated through the office. Daria listened to a favorite holiday song as she busied herself with all her usual morning routines, ignoring the oversize vase with flowers sitting in the middle of her blotter. She didn't have to look at the card. She knew who they were from. And the cold chill that knowledge gave her after yesterday's meeting with Detective Kevin Gordon left her raw.

"You're killing me," Marla finally shrieked, standing at the doorway with her arms crossed.

"Am I?"

"Someone leaves you these big, beautiful flowers and you're checking your in-box to see what's in store for the day? Forget it! You don't have any meetings. I already checked. Read the note already, will ya? I'm dying here."

She opened the card under Marla's watchful eye as her assistant dreamily touched one of the bright yellow-and-orange petals in the bouquet.

You'll always be my *pretty little bird.* She placed the card on the blotter and stole a glance at the flowers. The bird-of-paradise flowers were exquisitely arranged in tropical foliage in a crystal vase. Just the sight of them made her heart hammer in her chest—but with dread, not excitement.

"I would have expected a Christmas arrangement this time of year, but these are gorgeous," Marla said. "Must have cost whoever sent them a fortune."

"I'm sure."

Marla glanced at the writing on the card, which was visible since Daria had place it faceup. "Cryptic."

"Typical," Daria said.

"Typical? Are you kidding? Man, I'm so jealous." Marla's eyes twinkled. "So do you know who they're from?"

Daria glanced at Marla's knowing smirk.

Marla giggled. "They're from George. I think your ex might want a little holiday reunion with you," she said in a singsong voice.

She'd known immediately the flowers were from George, but just the mention of his name sent a trickle of fear through her. The intense urge to tear up the note and toss the flowers, vase and all, in the trash was overwhelming. But that would only end in questions from Marla.

Instead, she shoved the note into her trash can, got up from her desk chair and carried the vase to the credenza on the other side of her office.

"What are you doing?" Marla asked, watching in shock as Daria plopped the flowers on the credenza.

As she walked back to her desk, Daria said, "George and I are finished, Marla."

Marla bent down and looked at her squarely, her brown eyes flashing and her mouth agape. "Oh, wow, you're upset! You were expecting these to be from someone else, weren't you?" She pointed a well-manicured red-coated finger at Daria accusingly. "If you've been holding out on me about some secret boyfriend, you'd better spill, girl. I need details."

Daria rolled her eyes. "Get real, Marla. When do I ever have time for a man? If I'm not knee-deep in plaster dust, I'm pulling splinters out of my palms from hauling

wood to and from my truck." She hoped her unrest
didn't show on her face. But she needed to know. "How
did you know they were from George?"

Marla pursed her lips. "Because he strutted right by
me this morning as I was walking into the office. Looking
mighty fine, if you ask me. What other reason would he
have for being here if not to give you these flowers?"

It had been a long time since Daria had seen George.
Would he be so bold after the meeting he'd had with
Kevin the other night?

Daria didn't believe for one minute that George was
trying to win her back. He hadn't fought the divorce at
all, but he'd made it clear he was angry—deeply
angry—with her for initiating it. He'd always been all
about appearances. He hadn't cared about their marriage
so much as their appearance as a perfect couple.

It was so like George to care only about things that
other people thought were important, things that impressed. Throughout their marriage, he had been very
generous with gifts, even when things were at their
worst between them. Unfortunately, the very things
Daria had wanted—no, needed—were things George
hadn't been capable of giving.

In contrast, a man like Kevin Gordon had real depth.
She'd been surprised by his determination to watch over
her. It was such a contrast to the way that George, by
the end of their marriage, only ever thought of himself.
But even aside from George, how many men would do
what Kevin was doing for her? Sure, he was a police
officer, but even he said the department didn't have the
means to protect her.

No, what he was doing for her—however frustrating
it was to be smothered with his protection—came from

character. His motives were honest and without any interest in what he could get back in return. It was refreshing to meet someone so unselfish. And she knew she should be grateful for the protection he offered.

If George was determined to have her killed as he'd planned, she was going to need all the help she could get. Especially since he'd made it clear how easily he could get past security and breeze right into her office.

Daria glanced at Marla's wide eyes as she gazed longingly at the flowers. A man like George could easily impress a woman like Marla. And it was clear he had. Her assistant wouldn't be much of a roadblock if George came to the office again. But why today? Why would he send her these ridiculous flowers? Was he trying to scare her? If he was, he'd succeeded.

Regardless, his card said it all.

"What's today's date, Marla?"

Marla gave her a questioning look and tapped her fingers on the small day planner on the corner of her desk.

Daria stared at the planner and a chill raced up her spine, leaving her hands trembling. In that split second, she knew exactly what it meant. Divorced or not, George's intentions were clear. To him, she was still his property.

"Today would have been our anniversary."

FOUR

"Carlisle was in her office, Matt," Kevin boomed. He paced Captain Jorgensen's office in a fury, riding on a burst of adrenaline. Ever since Ski had called to tell him George Carlisle was seen leaving the grounds of the building where Daria worked, Kevin hadn't been able to keep still.

He'd left her there. Even knowing she could still be in danger, Kevin had watched her step out of her truck and make her way toward the building.

And all the while George Carlisle, the man Kevin was supposed to be protecting her from, was inside. Or had been. Maybe he'd already come and gone by the time Daria had made her way to her office. Kevin didn't know. But the man had been there.

And as he paced Captain Jorgensen's office, it irritated Kevin to no end that he didn't know a single thing about what had happened at her office building today. The only info he had was what Ski had reported to him shortly before roll call.

What was Daria thinking? He'd just told her her ex-husband was trying to have her murdered. Why hadn't she called him when George made contact?

The captain pulled the pen cap he'd been chewing out of his mouth. "We don't have an active restraining order to keep him away. Until we do, there's no law against George Carlisle dropping by his ex-wife's office. The building is open to the public. There have to be about thirty companies in that building. The man might have had legitimate business in any one of them."

"And maybe I'll sprout wings and fly like Tinker Bell," Kevin drawled.

"That would be a sight to see." There was no humor in the captain's voice.

"You don't really believe he was there on legitimate business, do you?"

"No. And neither do you," Jorgensen said. "But it doesn't matter what you or I believe. What matters is the law and as of right now George Carlisle has a free man's right to walk the streets as he pleases. His attorney made sure of that. Until that changes, until he's actually done something outside of his meeting with you the other night to warrant this attention you're giving him, there isn't a thing I can do."

Kevin ground to a halt. There were days when the boundaries that closed around him while on the job were frustrating.

Captain Matt Jorgensen, newly appointed as captain of the precinct only seven months ago, leaned forward and propped his elbows on his desk. He was a lean man, a good six to eight years older than Kevin, though he kept himself fit, so his years didn't show. His dark hair was slightly thinning on top in the way of a high forehead, but it didn't seem to bother the man.

His by-the-book code of policing, leaving no wiggle room where the law was concerned, had advanced him up the ranks of law enforcement ahead of cops with more policing experience than his own ten years. Kevin supposed his code was more from character than career advancement and was possibly the only way he'd been able to keep sane in a world that was sometimes so utterly out of order.

Very little was ever spoken about Matt Jorgensen's past. What little Kevin did know was usually talked about in hushed voices. The man had lost his wife in a brutal murder over ten years ago and he'd been fingered. Rumor was, the police hadn't even looked for another suspect. It had been Matt's own digging and relentless work with his attorney that eventually got him off the rap. But the case had grown cold and the killer was never found. Matt had gone to the academy soon after.

"Is Daria Carlisle looking to get a restraining order? Did she ask for your help?" Matt asked.

"No," Kevin reluctantly admitted. Which irritated him further. Daria had to have known George was at her office. Ski had seen Carlisle carrying flowers on his way into the building, but not on the way out. When she'd found the flowers, she should have called him.

"I told you before," Matt said, leaning back in his chair. "George Carlisle hasn't broken any laws. And he has a viper attorney who will strike at us if we even breathe George Carlisle's name the wrong way. Unless you want to get bitten, you need to back off. We have done all we can in this situation."

"I should have walked away from that meeting as soon as I heard the static in my piece. If I'd done the job right the other night, George Carlisle might be behind bars right now."

The captain's shoulders drooped in impatient form.

"'Might be' is the operative phrase. Look, we've been through all this."

"And none of us came out happy in the end. Least of all Daria Carlisle."

Matt threw his hands up by his side. "I don't hear Ms. Carlisle complaining. You told her what happened down at the salvage yard. You offered her a solution and she flat out rejected it. She hasn't called this office asking for help, as far as I know."

"Because she won't believe her ex is capable of murder," he drawled.

With a shrug, Matt said, "We've see that before. Are you really surprised?"

No, Kevin wasn't. He'd seen women run back to their husbands after a standoff with a loaded gun to their head.

Of course, he knew the reason why they did it. Some women simply refused to believe they were actually in danger. They chose to ignore the signs of trouble. He'd seen it firsthand, when his sister's best friend had been murdered. Lucy had believed she had nothing to fear from her ex-boyfriend. And now she was dead. How many women had he seen follow Lucy's path in the years he'd been on the force?

Too many, he decided. He didn't want it to be too late for Daria, as it had been for Lucy. It had been nearly twenty years since Lucy's death, but Daria's case brought all the fear and frustration back.

Daria wasn't Lucy. But she did need protection. And he wasn't going to let her down.

"We need department support to tail Carlisle. Between me, Jake and Ski, there aren't enough hours in the day."

"Or enough dollars in your bank account to personally pay off-duty officers." Matt shook his head and darted a pointed finger at Kevin. "Don't deny it—I don't want to discuss it. I don't even want to know what you, Santos and Stanasloski are doing on your off-hours. I have a feeling it'll just tick me off and I'm sure it won't make Carlisle's attorney any happier. And as far as getting the department to authorize the overtime, no can do. I just can't justify the expense to the commissioner.

"Look, you've always been focused on your job. In the seven months I've been here it's been clear something is driving you more than just the paycheck. I know what that's like," he said. Then Matt's attention turned to the people gathered in the hall outside his office door.

"We've got company," he said as he rose from the seat behind his desk. "Why do I have a feeling I'm not going to like this?"

Kevin threw open the door and stared into the cold eyes of George Carlisle's attorney. He was Lawrence Bingham, a partner at one of those uptown law firms with a string of names no one but the partners ever remembered. Kevin had met the man the previous morning when Bingham strode into the station in high-class loafers and Sunday casual clothes that probably cost more than a month of the average cop's salary. Kevin had never begrudged anyone with money. He'd always had enough to satisfy himself and figured most people worked for what they wanted or needed. But he'd never cared for people who flaunted their wealth as a way to set themselves above others.

"What is going on here?" Matt asked.

District Attorney Martha Landers stepped into the office beside Bingham, her expression tight.

Bingham's cool smile had just enough edge to be annoying. "That's what I'd like to know."

Martha sighed. "Mr. Bingham tells me one of your officers is harassing his client."

Matt shook his head. "We went over all this the other morning. My officers were doing their job."

"Does that include false arrest, too?"

"That arrest was perfectly legal," Kevin said firmly. "Textbook, even."

Matt nodded. "I agree. I've read the report. Detective Gordon had probable cause. The arrest was clean and as soon as the mistake was cleared up, your client was released without any harm."

Bingham laughed harshly. "I'm not here to debate what you perceive as probable cause these days. I'm talking about this morning when my client found one of your officers tailing him."

Jorgensen tossed a disgusted look at Kevin that might as well have been a flogging. Kevin was almost too surprised to notice. Ski was usually stealthlike when he was tailing someone. Despite his nervous twitch, he was good at keeping himself invisible. Carlisle hadn't seen him for the two weeks they'd been tailing him before the meeting. But obviously Carlisle was aware of them now and that meant they'd all have to be more careful.

"It's bad enough to be falsely accused, to have your reputation tarnished with innuendo. But to be stalked and made to fear the very people who've sworn to protect and serve, well…"

Kevin shoved his hands into his pockets in an attempt to give them something to do other than grab Bingham by the throat. Bingham was baiting Kevin. He wanted Kevin to lose his cool, act like a crazed cop to strengthen his case against the department and to give credence to George Carlisle's claim that he was being harassed. But he wasn't about to let Bingham get the best of him.

"My client had some banking business this morning and found Detective Gordon sitting outside the building when he came out."

Kevin quickly ran the events of the morning through his head. He hadn't seen Carlisle leaving the building after Daria went inside. He'd only waited long enough for Daria to enter the building before leaving himself. Ski had told him Carlisle was long gone before Daria had arrived. The only way Carlisle would have known Kevin had been there was if he'd come back.

"I was doing my job, which is to protect Ms. Carlisle from your client," he told Bingham.

Martha cocked her head. "So you were at Ms. Carlisle's office building this morning?"

"Yes."

Bingham flipped his hand. "There. He's admitted to stalking my client. I want charges brought against Detective Gordon and a restraining order issued. I won't tolerate Gordon harassing my client any longer."

"He's done no such thing," Martha said firmly, shifting her briefcase from one hand to the other. She shook a head of short salt-and-pepper curls in impatience. "And none of this will hold up in court. You and I both know that, Mr. Bingham. I will also not entertain any notion of false arrest on this matter. I've seen the report. The officers at the salvage yard believed they had probable cause for an arrest. The department released your client as soon as they discovered there was no evidence on that tape. Your client should be happy they didn't hold him the full forty-eight hours the law allows."

Bingham huffed. "Regardless, I want to file a restraining order against this officer."

"For what?" Matt said. "He's already stated his reason for being at Ms. Carlisle's office building was for her protection. It had nothing to do with your client."

Martha turned to Kevin. "Will Ms. Carlisle verify that you were there on her behalf?"

"We spoke this morning and I told her that I'd follow her to make sure she got into her office safely."

"That's ridiculous." Bingham huffed. "This has been very distressing for Mr. Carlisle, and the notion—"

"Poor guy," Kevin drawled. "Plotting murder always takes a lot out of a man."

"The notion my client would be harmful to his wife is absurd." Bingham sliced Kevin with an icy glare. "You hauled an innocent man off the streets and subjected him to brutality. As of this point, you're on notice. If anyone in this department crosses the line and harasses my client again, I'll make sure you all lose your badges."

Matt rolled his eyes, clearly having reached the limit of his patience. "My officers will continue to act in the best interests of the public and if in doing that they so happen to step on your client's toes—"

"Then it's too bad," Kevin interjected.

"If you so much as come near my client—"

"I have no intention of stepping one foot near your client," Kevin warned, taking a step closer. "But you can tell him for me that I will be glued to his ex-wife from now on to make sure nothing happens to her. And if anything does, I'll personally be hunting him down for that arrest."

With a haughty lift of his chin, Bingham spun on his

heel and strode away without looking back. It took a moment before anyone spoke.

"That went well," Martha said flatly with a tight smile, brushing the imaginary dust Bingham had left in his wake off the lapel of her navy suit. "Daria Carlisle did agree to having surveillance, Detective Gordon? Didn't she?"

He sighed. "Not in so many words."

Matt gave him a sidelong glance. "Exactly what words did she use?"

Kevin stole a quick glance at the district attorney, who quickly waved him off and said, "I have a feeling I don't want to know."

As Daria approached the house and pulled into the driveway she saw Kevin's truck parked at the curb. He was waiting for her. She didn't have to fear her ex-husband. Kevin's scowl alone was enough to stop her dead in her tracks.

"Where have you been? You said you were going to be home around six."

"Hello to you, too." She leaned across the bench seat and picked up the flowers and glass vase.

Kevin's eyes fixed on the flowers, his stare intense, before he lifted his eyes to her. The intensity of his gaze never waned.

She ignored his chilling look. She missed that fun-loving smile Kevin had had at the market. That would have been nice to come home to after the miserable day she'd had at work.

"When were you going to tell me?"

She feigned ignorance. "About what?"

His jaw squared. "You know what I'm talking about. Carlisle came to see you today."

She couldn't quite put a finger on what annoyed her more, greeting him when they were both in such a foul mood, or the fact that her ex-husband was all Kevin seemed to care about where she was concerned.

"I wasn't," she answered honestly. "He was long gone before I arrived at work. I didn't think it was necessary to tell you."

She'd thought about it all day, endlessly. She was a person who loved her job, prided herself on her work. But the number of mistakes she'd made today from sheer distraction over this stupid vase of flowers had her fed up about the entire ridiculous situation. She didn't want to think about George or these flowers anymore. She wanted it to be three days ago before Kevin had that stupid meeting with George at the salvage yard. When her life was normal and she could happily work on her house and do her job without distraction.

"You're not making this easy, Daria."

"It isn't easy any way you look at it."

"If you don't care about your own safety, how can you expect the police to keep you safe? Didn't you hear anything I told you yesterday?"

"More than you realize."

She thought she'd said the words under her breath, but the immediate reaction that registered in Kevin's expression told her otherwise.

"Look, I heard everything you said. And I've worked the situation backward and forward and every other way I could. I did it last night and then again at the office. The bottom line is, I can't leave even if I want to. I need my paycheck to get by. I don't have any money in savings. At least nothing that will last more than a few days. I have no place to go. No one to go to now that my parents are in Mexico. I'm stuck here whether you and I like it or not."

After Kevin left her yesterday, she'd spent the day second-guessing her decision to stay in the house. So much so that her head hurt. But there was nothing she could do. She had no extra money in the bank and only enough room on her credit card to pay for about a week's stay at a hotel. And not even a good hotel.

She'd used up all her vacation time over the summer working on the house's plumbing and she wasn't going to get any more vacation pay until January first—nearly four more weeks until she could arrange vacation leave. Even then, she only had three weeks' worth of vacation time each year before she'd have to take unpaid time.

She blew out a breath of frustration and felt the tears that she'd held back most of the day push to the surface. Admitting her true situation out loud to Kevin had been harder than she'd imagined. She was stuck and it was her desire to finally own a home of her own that had put her there.

A sudden chill invaded her body. Looking at him squarely, she pushed the car door shut and held up the flowers. "I need to get rid of these. I don't want them in my house."

With a little extra effort, Daria walked up the path, her heart pounding in her chest. She'd half thought of keeping these flowers at work, giving them to a coworker. They were beautiful, and it seemed a shame to just throw them out. But every time she'd looked at them, it was like George was right there in the office with her.

She'd found herself on the phone with clients staring at the enormous, colorful bouquet and picturing herself lying on the ground in some dark alley, bleeding to death. She'd nearly jumped half a mile high when Marla had walked into her office and tapped on her shoulder.

Bringing the flowers home and dumping them into her compost pile seemed like the best solution. If she'd dumped them at work, people would talk. Marla certainly would ask questions. The last thing she needed was for people to start gossiping at work.

"He was in your office, Daria."

"Yes, he was. But like I said, I didn't see him. He came and left before I even arrived at work."

"He left you a card? Is that how you knew these were from him?"

"There was an unsigned card. But I knew it was him. My assistant saw him leaving the building. And anyway, he always bought me bird-of-paradise bouquets."

Not wanting to discuss it anymore, she walked past him. He followed on her heels to the end of the driveway.

"Look, I'm tired," she said. "It was a long day."

Kevin didn't say anything more, but the questions were there in his expression. He slipped his hands into the pockets of his blue jeans and stood in the driveway watching her as she walked to the backyard, where she kept her compost pile. Dropping her lunch bag and purse to the pavement, she gripped the vase a little tighter and clumsily stalked across the grass as the heels of her pumps sank into the soft, wet earth.

Building a compost pile out of chicken-wire fencing and stakes had been easy when she'd first moved in and began working on the yard. All her grass clippings and organic kitchen waste, from eggshells to vegetable peelings, would one day turn into rich soil to feed her gardens. All she had to do was till them under and let them bake in the hot sun. These flowers would turn to good soil, too, once nature had a chance to do its work.

When she reached the compost pile, she lifted the thin, black sheathing she used to cover the pile. With a quick turn of her hands, Daria dumped the contents of the vase into the pile of vegetation already there and replaced the sheathing.

Rubbing the dirt and wetness off her fingertips, she decided she'd till the whole pile over the weekend. It would get a little frustration worked out of her system. In truth, she could use that kind of workout tonight, but her muscles ached and her emotions were shot.

She retrieved her purse and lunch bag from the end of the driveway and stopped when she heard movement deep in the back of the property. Her heart raced, and she turned back to the house, taking in the eerie blackness of it. She never left any of the inside lights on during the day while she wasn't home. It had never bothered her to walk into a dark house before. But suddenly walking inside seemed unnerving.

She shook her head and chided her foolishness. This was her home. She refused to be afraid of it.

"You may want to think about adding some floodlights with motion detectors to the front and back yard," Kevin said, still waiting for her in the driveway. "Something with a cage around the light so the neighborhood kids can't pick it off with a rock. Sometimes that's all it takes to distract prowlers. Which reminds me, your front-porch light has been smashed."

"It has?"

"Yeah, that's why I'm mentioning the cage. You have busy kids in this neighborhood."

"I'll say. My bank account is taking a beating

between the graffiti and the broken lights. Thanks for the suggestion. But why do I need floodlights out front if you're going to be here barking at me every night?"

She waited for him to move. Kevin stood for a moment, staring at her in the darkness. If there was a big yellow moon hanging low in the sky she would be able to see the strong features of Kevin's face. There was something commanding about the way he looked at her, strong and sure of himself. No woman need fear for herself in his presence.

But there was no yellow moon and now no bright lights from her porch shining down on them. There wasn't even a lone car with bright headlights driving down her street. And even if she could see Kevin's face, she had a good idea of the scowl he was wearing.

"How come you don't use the front door? Even with the light out you'd be able to see with the street lamp."

"And you'd be able to see me, too."

"Exactly. I want to make sure you get inside okay. But seriously, the front porch is closer to where you park your car."

"My front-door lock sticks sometimes. I could spend fifteen minutes just wiggling the key in the dead bolt on a cold night. After the day I've had, I really don't need to wrestle with it." Rolling her eyes, she added, "But if it would make you feel any better to watch me go into the yard with a little bit of light, Detective, I'll grab the flashlight from my truck."

"I'm not going to feel better until I get George Carlisle in jail."

"Well, I can't help you there." She grabbed the flashlight from the glove box and turned it on. "I'm all set. Good night, Detective."

Kevin nodded, then turned and walked back to his SUV while she headed to the backyard. She felt a brief pang at the thought of him sitting out there in the dark and cold all night, but she pushed it away. If Kevin Gordon wanted to waste his time watching her house and every move she made, that was his business. Daria wasn't going to feel guilty about it.

As she walked toward the back porch, she stole a glance up at the sky. The weather report she'd heard on the drive home said they'd be getting snow. And Kevin would be sleeping in his car.

Expelling a defeated sigh, she climbed the stairs. Juggling her purse, lunch bag, vase and the flashlight, she couldn't reach the door handle, so she stuck the flashlight tightly under her arm and yanked at the screen door with her free hand. As she shone the light back on the door to get her key in the lock, she froze.

The glass vase slipped from her fingers and fell to the floorboards, crashing and spraying a million tiny shards around her feet. The beam of the flashlight hung like a spotlight on a stage performer, making the eyes of the large, dead bird hanging from a thin wire from her door knocker glow. One wing of the bird was twisted awkwardly to one side while the other lay flat against its side. Its talons hung limp as if it were hanging from a gallows.

Daria took a wide step back. With each step she felt the fragments of glass crunch beneath her shoes. All her breath rushed out of her lungs with a whoosh. As she clutched her hands to her chest, she was vaguely aware that someone was screaming.

FIVE

Kevin stalked back to his truck, fuming about stubborn women. *Lord, give me patience with this one.* He'd somewhat come to terms with the willfulness of the opposite sex years ago while growing up in the same house as his sister, but no woman had ever riled him like Daria Carlisle.

As soon as he'd reached the curb, he turned to watch for the inside light to turn on. Spot started barking again, as he'd done when Kevin first arrived, pulling his attention away from the house. The urgency of the bark put Kevin on alarm. That's when he heard movement coming from the backyard.

Daria's high-pitched scream pealed through the darkness. Kevin's blood turned to ice as he ran toward the back porch, his heart pumping wildly, his ears ringing with the sound of her scream.

When he turned the corner at the end of the driveway, he found Daria standing on the back porch, hugging the railing with the empty vase shattered at her feet.

As Kevin raced up the stairs, Daria flew into his arms, trembling. "What happened? Are you all right?"

He couldn't see her face. Clutching her arms, he

forced her to look up at him and as she did, a small sob escaped her lips.

"I—I opened th-the door," she sobbed, bending one arm behind her toward the house.

He didn't need to move any closer. With the light from the flashlight in her hand shining on the door, he could see what looked like a bird hanging in a noose behind the screen door. At first glance, it didn't look any more dangerous than a stuffed scarecrow hanging on the door in autumn as decoration. But this was no toy.

Daria clung to him, even as he took a wide stride forward to take a closer look at the dead bird. There was no note, no obvious signs of damage to the door. Just what appeared to be a dead crow hanging from a wire.

The hairs on the back of his head stood on end when Spot's bark became more urgent. Kevin couldn't see the dog, but heard the dog chain scraping over Mrs. Hildebrand's concrete-block patio as he tried to pull free. A gust of wind blew strong and the noise in the backyard he'd originally thought was Daria now sounded too close to the house for comfort.

"Get in my truck and lock the door," Kevin said, staring into the backyard. "And once you're there, don't move, do you hear me? You stay there until I get back."

"Where are you going?"

"I just want to check around the house."

She hiccupped a sob. "I don't want to be alone."

"Go to the truck, Daria. I just need to check around the back and see if whoever did this is still here."

"Please don't go," she whispered.

"You'll be okay. Just get into my truck and lock the door."

Although she hesitated, Daria nodded.

She ran down the stairs toward the street. Once she was out of view, Kevin moved in the opposite direction toward the backyard and into the shadows.

The door to Kevin's truck was unlocked and Daria climbed in quickly, shutting and locking the door behind her. But for some reason, she couldn't sit still. She felt too vulnerable, too exposed, and she really didn't want to sit out in the dark all alone. She needed comfort. She needed to feel safe and that could only happen after she went inside her home and locked all her doors.

Slipping back out of the SUV she walked to the front porch. In contrast to the back of the house, the front porch was well lit enough for her to see what she was doing and see anyone around her. She'd have to fight with the front lock again, but she wouldn't have to deal with being alone in the dark until Kevin came back.

She struggled with her shaking hands to get the key in the lock, then fought to get it to turn. Tears sprang to her eyes, her shoulders sagging. She'd just replaced the lock last week! Obviously she'd done something wrong or the lock would work right. What would she do if she couldn't get it open, if she was stuck out here on the porch, completely unprotected?

Sniffing, she jiggled the key up and down as she turned the doorknob. Relief washed over her when it finally turned and the door opened.

Once inside, Daria threw on the light switches by the door, illuminating the antique hanging lamp that lit up her stairway and the hall leading to the living room and kitchen. Without pulling off her coat, she moved down the hallway and switched on all the rest of the lights in the house until every room was lit up like a Christmas tree.

Her insides trembled. Instinctively she hugged her coat tightly around her. But even as she did, Daria knew that wouldn't make a difference. The cold wind that swept through her had nothing to do with the temperature in the house.

The front door swung open, creaking on its hinges, and she leaped.

"Someone was out there, but he's long gone now," Kevin said, to her utter relief. "I thought I told you to stay in my truck. I got worried when I didn't see you in there."

"I didn't want to be alone outside."

"You should have let me check the house first," Kevin said gently. "Whoever left the bird could have gotten inside."

Daria's eyes widened as her jaw dropped. "Are you purposely trying to scare me?"

"No. Just trying to be cautious."

"Did you actually see anyone in my backyard?"

"I heard something, but I didn't see anyone. But usually when someone is bold enough to pull a prank like hanging a dead bird on someone's door, they wait around for the reaction."

She laughed without humor. "Well, if someone was watching, they got a good reaction out of me."

His shoulders sagged. "This whole thing reeks of a prank from street kids."

"You sound like you're disappointed."

"Suspicious. I'm not crazy about the idea of it being common knowledge that you use the back door, in the dark, but that just makes it all the more likely it's someone from the neighborhood. George was planning to hire a hit man to take you out—he'd have no reason to do surveillance on you himself. Besides, from the amount of complaints I found that were filed from this neighborhood, these kids have been causing trouble for a while. This could be one more prank."

Daria straightened her posture. "Say it. You don't believe it was them."

Kevin glanced around the room, his face still wearing the scowl she knew he'd had earlier. "I don't know. I prefer the street-kids explanation, but I don't want to overlook anything that might lead back to George. Why would your ex leave a bird on your door? And on a day he also sends you flowers?"

"The note on the card that came with the flowers said 'You'll always be *my* pretty little bird' with an emphasis on the word *my.* George always called me his pretty little bird. Now there's a dead bird on my door." She shook her head. "This is crazy. George would never touch a dead bird. He's obsessed with germs. He even donates blood and stores it just in case he needs it for an operation, because he's afraid of getting someone else's tainted blood."

It felt good to talk. Not about George but just to fill the quiet with noise. Kevin seemed oblivious to her need for chatter as he moved around the rooms, searching downstairs. He then stopped in the hallway and dialed a number on his cell phone.

He was being professional and she appreciated that. Kevin was, after all, a police officer. He wasn't there to make her feel better. Her knee-jerk reaction to run into his arms earlier had been an emotional response.

"Where's Carlisle?" he growled into his phone. Kevin listened for a few minutes, then talked a little more to whomever it was he'd called. Daria wasn't listening. She was glancing around the rooms at all that she'd created, and all she'd envisioned this house could be.

She'd never imagined someone would breach the safety of her home and she hoped there was no evidence that anyone had gotten inside. Anger surged through her, replacing the heart-pounding fear.

After stalking to the front door, Daria tried the knob. It turned easily enough from the inside. She turned the dead bolt with added pressure. It squeaked, but slipped into place. Perhaps all it would take would be a few drops of oil to remedy the problem. She could fix that. Daria could fix lots of things.

"Ski's had your ex under his nose for the past hour. Whoever was out there, it wasn't him. That should make you rest easier tonight," he said as he folded his cell phone and slipped it back into his pocket. There was a deep crease in his brow.

"What kind of kids do something like this?"

"I know you're upset, and rightly so, but sticking a crow on the door was probably some kind dare for some junior-high-school kid out to have a little fun. Scaring up trouble by scaring you was probably all they were after."

That should have put her at ease, but it didn't. She closed her eyes, turning away from Kevin. She wanted to believe it was a street thug trying to spook her. But it seemed rather brazen to think they'd leave her a dead animal like that. But regardless of who was responsible, her response would be the same—nothing. There wasn't anything she could do.

"What is it?" Kevin asked, his brows furrowing with suspicion.

She'd never felt stuck before, but like it or not, she was stuck here now. The feeling wasn't very appealing, but it was reality.

"Nothing," she said, rubbing her hands over her face. "It's just been a long day and I didn't get a lot of sleep last night."

"You and me both. Ski's coming over with a crew to dust the back porch. Maybe we'll get lucky and find some fingerprints. If this joker's been brought in before, he'll have a file that will help us ID him."

"Whoever did this wasn't a boy," she said, not wanting to admit it. "Boys don't terrorize people that way."

He smiled crookedly. Small as it was, it did wonders to put her at ease. She liked it when he smiled. His voice was low and quiet when he spoke. "Daria, I was a boy once. Sometimes the highlight of my day was getting my sister, Judy, and her friends to scream by playing some prank."

"You?"

Kevin laughed then and for the first time that evening, she felt herself coming back. It was going to be okay.

"Much as I'd love to blame this on your ex as a way to nail him, I can't. He wasn't anywhere near your house today and it doesn't seem likely he'd have been able to convince some kids to do the deed without Ski having seen him talk to them. The clowns who did this are probably down at the park having a good laugh about the whole thing."

"At my expense," she said, chuckling nervously. "Is that what you used to do?"

He shrugged. "I was no angel."

Sighing, she said, "This has just shaken me a bit. I've

always suspected that some of the kids who used to party here might not have heard the house was sold, and that they might come back for some mischief."

"It's very obvious the house isn't abandoned anymore."

She glanced at him, saw the dark shadow that seemed to cross his face and knew he wasn't going to let the subject go.

"It couldn't have been George. But I can't help thinking about the flowers and the note. The flowers George sent me were birds-of-paradise."

His expression was blank. "And?"

She walked to the counter and leaned against it. She needed the distance, if only for the few extra feet it afforded.

"George proposed to me at a place called the Paradise Inn. At one time, it used to be our restaurant. We would go there for special occasions. They had these silk flowers on every table."

"Where are you going with this?"

"They were birds-of-paradise. Just like the ones I got today. Today would have been our anniversary." She cleared her throat and looked down at her cruddy linoleum floor.

Kevin nodded. "That would explain why he chose those flowers then. But sending them on your anniversary...I don't understand that."

"If he was still carrying some kind of torch for me, I could see it," Daria said. "But when I filed for divorce, he made it very clear that everything would be over between us if I walked out that door. He said he couldn't forgive my 'betrayal.'"

"Do you think that's what this is about?"

She snapped her gaze to him as she nervously kicked

a worn patch of linoleum on the floor. "How do you mean?"

Kevin took a small step toward her. "Maybe he's planned this as revenge?"

She frowned. "I thought he'd already gotten his revenge with the divorce settlement. I was left with next to nothing—I figured that would satisfy him. But when I saw the flowers today, I started to wonder. If this is his way of showing he can still get to me, in spite of you— if this is his way of scaring me, then it's working."

She stared at the spot on the floor she'd been worrying. The pressure of tears behind her eyes made them ache. She didn't want to spend her days picking at the significance of every moment she'd spent with George to see if he had always been this cold, this frightening. When had the man she loved turned into this monster? Was he truly capable of hiring her murderer? Could she really have been that blind?

Daria folded her arms across her chest, breathing deeply while she felt her pulse easing and her heartbeat growing steady.

She waved off the thoughts flooding her mind.

"I thought I was beyond my marriage. Starting over. But I've been doubting a lot of things lately. All I know is that the problems with neighborhood kids causing trouble around here didn't start when I moved in. It's been going on for years. But I've never heard of something like this happening before."

"Even if this wasn't your ex-husband's doing, you're still not safe here." Kevin lifted an eyebrow, emotions she couldn't quite decipher racing across his face. "Have you thought any more about leaving?"

"Did you hear anything I said outside? I don't have

the money to just pick up and leave. All my money is tied up in this place."

Shame enveloped her for the predicament she'd put herself in. She should have kept a reserve of money aside the way she had when she'd been saving for the house. That money was long gone now. If she'd had even a portion of it, she could use it to get by at least until her vacation pay kicked in. Admitting how dire her financial situation was to Kevin only made her feel worse.

"I spent all of last night trying to figure out a way to go away even for a little while. But I can't keep up the house payment and upkeep here *and* afford to stay at a motel somewhere else. As it is, my paycheck barely covers my personal expenses, and what little is left over goes to building supplies."

"Can't you ask your parents for a loan?"

Daria laughed softly. "My parents live a very modest lifestyle. Right now they're not even in the country. Where they're staying they don't even have a phone."

"I see."

"No," she said, "I don't think you really do. But it doesn't matter. I'm going to go into my bedroom, find a nice comfortable pair of sweats and then go take a long, hot bubble bath in my big claw-foot tub. It's been a long day. I think I'm due."

Kevin's crystal eyes stared back at her with sympathy and it shamed her. Did he believe her to be as much a failure as she felt right then? She was an accountant. She knew better than to leave herself exposed without any money in reserve for emergencies.

Daria dragged her gaze from him. She wanted to know what he was thinking as his eyes grazed the windowpane, but she was afraid to ask. Was he angry with her for the position he seemed to be in, feeling as if his life was on hold because she refused to leave?

But instead of scolding her or making judgments, he said, "You may be more comfortable holding off on that bath until the boys have had a chance to dust the porch."

She held his gaze for as long as she could stand it. In the end, she wasn't as strong as Kevin. Daria finally nodded and walked to the bedroom.

Kevin was still watching her as she closed her bedroom door. *Such fortitude, such strength,* she thought. As irritating as this situation was, his steadfastness was something she admired about Kevin. It was a quality she'd hoped to find in a life partner some day in the future. If she'd met Kevin under other circumstances, she'd be thinking of the possibility that this man could be something more than her protector. He could be part of her future.

It looked as if George had destroyed her chance at that, as well.

SIX

The "boys" had come and gone. Kevin had left the house along with them. Scrubbed clean from her bath, Daria paced the bedroom in her slippers, sleep eluding her again. It was hard enough to handle the idea that someone had come to her house with the express purpose of trying to scare her. But knowing that Kevin felt the need to stay outside her door to protect her from that danger was unsettling.

The wind rattled through the rafters of her old house, finding the drafts and holes she'd put on her list to fix eventually. In a few short months spring would tease the air again and she'd be able to get to her to-do list. But right now the temperature outside was freezing, and the wind howled like a lone wolf in the distance. The cold wind, along with the quiet creak of the floorboards beneath her feet, only made her more restless.

After slipping into an old, comfortable terry-cloth robe, Daria pulled open the lid of the trunk at the foot of her bed and grabbed the extra blanket she kept stashed there, before heading to the kitchen. She poured the mixture of hot chocolate she'd prepared into a thermos and screwed on the lid, sealing it tight and capping it off with a cup.

There was nothing like a delicious cup of hot chocolate to keep a cold and sleep-deprived person warm. Kevin would probably collapse in the middle of roll call if he had to endure one more sleepless night. But at least he wouldn't be as cold tonight with some hot liquid warming his insides. It was the least she could do, since she knew that with Kevin sitting in front of the house the likelihood of someone coming back tonight was nil.

Besides, Daria couldn't stomach looking at her finances again. Her head ached from running numbers and coming up short every time. A walk in the fresh air would do her some good. Maybe even help settle her nerves so she could sleep.

It was nearly 1:00 a.m. and the temperature had dropped well below freezing. The nightly weather report warned of an added drop of ten degrees due to windchill. Snow was coming, even if it hadn't started yet.

After she gave Kevin the blanket and hot chocolate, she'd climb into bed and try to get some rest. If sleep didn't come soon she'd be barely coherent in the morning. Marla would throw a million and one questions filled with innuendo her way and Daria wasn't quite prepared to deal with that another day. She'd had her fill today every time Marla had come into her office and glanced at those stupid flowers.

Her assistant had always liked George, a fact that had been evident when George had visited the office before Daria had filed for divorce. Daria had always known George's flash and position were things he prided himself on, as well as assets that drew women to him.

Being an outgoing woman, Marla had her pick of male suitors. But it was more than just envy over the flowers this morning that had Marla gazing longingly into Daria's office. Daria had always suspected that all it would take would be a tiny nudge, and Marla would make a move on George.

The sour feeling that churned in her stomach wasn't jealousy, but deep concern. While they were not close, Marla had been a good friend at work while Daria had gone through her emotional and legal trials. If George was capable of hiring someone to murder her, then no woman was safe with him. It would be easy for Marla to get caught up in a web from which she couldn't untangle herself.

Grabbing her jacket, Daria decided she wouldn't think about it now. Marla was a big girl and Daria neither had nor wanted control of the men her assistant chose to date. Daria had her own life and problems to deal with. Including the man camped out in front of her house.

Throwing open the front door, she stepped outside into the bitter cold, clutching the blanket in her arms as she moved down the stairs. The icy breeze shocked her skin and bit through the threads of her jacket. The trees lining the street creaked in protest against the wind and cold. A lone dog barked on the next block, and Daria practically jumped out of her skin.

Quickening her step, Daria hurried down the driveway to where Kevin was parked at the curb, expecting to find him sitting fitfully asleep in the front of his truck.

The truck was empty.

"Kevin?" she called out in a heavy whisper. A chill rocketed through her as she swung around, searching the darkness with widened eyes.

At the heavy bark of the dog on the next block, she twisted her body yet again, her arms nearly dropping the blanket and thermos in her hands. From inside Mrs.

Hildebrand's house, Spot came to life, adding in what sounded like a round-robin between the two animals. In the distance, another dog added to the chorus.

"What are you doing out here?"

Even knowing the sound of Kevin's voice, Daria still yelped. He had to have been walking on air, because she hadn't heard his approach. She'd been distracted by the dogs and her own rampant imagination.

Clutching the blanket and the thermos to her chest, she said, "Don't sneak up on me like that! You nearly gave me a heart attack."

"What are you doing out of the house this time of night? It could be dangerous. For a minute, I thought you were a prowler."

"I'm sorry," she said.

Kevin appeared oblivious to her annoyance. He waved the flashlight he gripped in his hands back and forth through the yard, sometimes looking at her, sometimes seeming to look through her, as if she weren't even there.

She cleared her throat. "I didn't mean to scare you."

He glanced at her then and his gaze held. "You didn't," he said quietly. "I heard the dogs barking and thought I'd check the yard. You must have come out the front door while I was in the backyard."

"I can open the front door easily enough from the inside. It's only from the outside that I have a hard time."

"Are you okay?"

Taken aback by the sudden concern in his voice, Daria shrugged and said, "I'm fine. I was just having trouble sleeping. The house has a lot of drafts and the wind gets pretty loud at night."

Kevin went back to panning the surrounding yards

with his flashlight. "Do the dogs always make this much noise?"

"Sometimes. We don't get a lot of stray dogs in this part of the city, but there are cats, and that's pretty much all Spot needs to see outside to start barking."

Kevin turned to her with a weak smile and flicked off the flashlight. "And once one starts, they all join in." His eyes were glassy from being hit with the cold wind. But the black jacket with the Providence PD emblem on it looked bulky and warm.

The mist from Kevin's breath escaped his mouth as he spoke, then evaporated instantly. The collar of his jacket was flipped up to protect his neck from the biting wind. Even with the jacket, he had to be cold, adding to the guilt Daria felt, but he didn't let on any discomfort.

"Tonight is a little more frigid than it's been in the last few days so I brought you a blanket and hot chocolate." She thrust the blanket and thermos out to him.

"If you insist on freezing yourself out here like this, it's the least I can do," she added when all he did was stare at her.

"You made me hot chocolate?"

"Yes. It's not homemade or anything. Just instant with a little bit of the half-and-half I bought the other day."

Kevin let out a slow sigh and reached for the carafe. "Oh, man, I think I love you."

Daria blinked, and then laughed. "No wonder Mrs. Hildebrand made you cookies. If you go around saying things like that to sweet-talk women, you'll be fattened up before Christmas."

"No, really. This is great. The coffee I got earlier is long gone. This should keep me warm tonight."

"Well, the blanket should keep you a little more comfortable. It's not electric or anything but it is wool. It kept me warm many nights when I didn't have any heat. Oh, here. Take it," she said as she shoved the blanket into his arms.

Kevin's smile was so bright it had her heart beating rampantly. It was only a blanket and some hot chocolate, after all. But he was grinning at her as if she'd given him the grand prize at a carnival.

Her arms were now empty. She crossed them in front of her chest to give them something to do. "It's just, I won't be able to sleep at all tonight if I think you're freezing out here. I don't know why. It's your decision to be here like this. Not mine."

He adjusted the blanket in his arms and repositioned the flashlight. A slow smile played at the corner of his lips as he gazed down at her.

"What are you smiling about?"

Kevin lifted his shoulder in a slight shrug. "Nothing. It was just a really nice thing for you to do, giving me a blanket. And the hot chocolate, too. Thanks."

His eyes never left hers and Daria didn't know what to say to him. He was wearing her down, getting her used to having him around. And that wasn't good at all. Although she had to admit that she'd been glad Kevin was there when she'd seen that bird on her door, she had to remind herself why Kevin was really there. It had nothing to do with her, he just wanted to catch George. When the danger left, he would, too. She couldn't let herself get attached, no matter how hard it was to remember to keep her distance when he smiled at her like that.

She cleared her throat, amazed that the words she was about to say were harder to say than she'd rehearsed in the house. "Then you should note for the record that

I think you've made your point and that staying here like this is ridiculous. You're insane if you think you can possibly keep up for very long working all day and staying up all night watching my house. This is my problem. Not yours."

"You're worried about me?"

"Don't change the subject."

"I thought I was the subject a few seconds ago. You're worried about how I'm holding up? Well, I'll tell you. It's not easy. But I know it's the right thing to do. Your ex-husband is quiet now, but the next time he makes a move, he's coming after you. And since I'm a police officer in this city, that makes it very much my problem, too."

She trembled with a gust of wind and she pulled her robe tighter. "This whole thing is insane."

"I can't really argue with that. But your decision to stay really leaves me no choice."

A fingernail of irritation scraped up her spine. Not at Kevin, but at her own predicament. "I've already told you I can't go."

His expression softened to something warm and caring and did loads to disintegrate her frustration.

"Yes, you did. I know it took a lot for you to admit that to me earlier. I'm glad you did. At least I know you understand the potential danger you're in right now, and you're not just being stubborn."

Surprised, she cocked her head. "Is that what you thought?"

"Initially, yes. A lot of women are in this situation."

"I'm not stupid, Kevin. I'd get out of danger if I could. I just feel stuck. I'm surprised you didn't know this already."

"About the money? No. I checked out the basics on you, but despite what most people think, the police can't check your bank account without a warrant. There was no justification to check yours."

Shifting in place to keep the cold from making her shudder, she said, "How basic? Do you have my SAT scores and elementary school records on file?"

He smiled. "You did really well in math. It's no wonder you went into accounting."

Her mouth dropped open.

"I'm kidding," he said with a chuckle.

She couldn't help laughing, too, but the seriousness of her situation soon took over.

"It wasn't your fault," she finally said. "You're not responsible."

He made a small grunt as if he was uncomfortable with her perceptiveness. "That's not the way I see it. And whether it is my fault or not, it is my responsibility. That's why I became a cop."

Daria sighed softly. "Good night, Kevin," she said and turned away from him.

He wouldn't sleep tonight because he was a man on a mission. She wouldn't sleep tonight either, but for an entirely different reason. And that reason would be the man, not the cop, staring at her window.

The next morning Daria fried an extra egg and slapped it on a toasted bagel with a few slices of bacon. She wasn't trying to impress Kevin, she told herself. She'd cooked for men before. Well, okay, it was only her father and her ex, but that counted, didn't it? It was only a stupid breakfast sandwich. And it wasn't like she was going out of her way to make it, either. She was making one for herself, too.

Frost had grown on the windowpane overnight, stretching crystal fingers that made it hard to look out the window, but she knew Kevin would still be there.

Slipping her feet into her boots, Daria wrapped the sandwich in wax paper and tossed it into a brown bag. She'd bring the sandwich out to Kevin and then start her truck to warm it up before leaving.

She stepped outside using the front door even though she'd have to come back in this way and lock the door from the inside before she left for work. Still, if she could possibly avoid the back door for a little bit longer, she would.

It was irrational. Daria knew she'd get over it in time, but for right now, it felt too raw.

Kevin rolled down the window as she approached.

"Good morning, sunshine," he said with a smile that instantly warmed her insides despite the frosty morning.

Feeling flattered, Daria smiled stupidly and held out the bag with the sandwich. As she did, she saw the plate of muffins on the seat next to him and her spirits fell. Hilda had beaten her to the punch.

Suddenly annoyed, she huffed, and pulled back her hand.

Kevin just gave her a sleepy grin. "What's that? Did you make something for me?"

"I thought you might be hungry, but I guess you're all set."

"No way. I can smell what's in that bag and it smells great."

Kevin reached his arm out through the open window to grab the bag. Daria tossed it to him. "If you keep eating all the baked goodies Mrs. Hildebrand gives you, you're going to get crumbs all over your seats."

A slow smile crept into the corner of his mouth. "Climb in. We can eat our breakfast together."

"I can't. I have to finish getting ready for work. But if you want to warm up in the house while you're eating, you're free to do so."

"Nah, it's okay. You look like you're almost ready to go and I don't want to get in your way." He opened the bag and breathed in the scent of the breakfast she'd made with longing. "My sister would be appalled. Judy tells me just one of these breakfast sandwiches has about three days' worth of fat, and that eating it clogs your arteries in a matter of minutes."

"Oh, really?"

"It's what she says."

"Since you're so concerned with your health I guess I'll toss it in the garbage."

He pulled the bag out of Daria's way as she reached in to grab it. "My sister is the health nut of the family. Not me."

"I'm surprised you're even still hungry. Mrs. Hildebrand seems to be keeping you well fed."

"I'm a guy. We're always hungry. Besides, Mrs. H. found my weakness. I lived my whole life having to eat my sister's granola biscuits and wheat-germ cookies just to please my mother. Who ever heard of putting wheat germ in cookies? Mrs. Hildebrand's muffins are amazing."

Terrific. Upstaged by muffins.

It was a distressing start to what stood to be a very frustrating day. Trying to obtain an unsecured personal loan without any real equity in her house, stocks or other assets was going to be tough. But if she was going to be able to get away from George for any length of time and stop all this nonsense, she'd have to break down and at least try to get a loan. If she was really careful, she might be able to stay in a room somewhere and still be able to pay her mortgage for a couple of months until she could think of a way out of this mess.

Daria shifted uncomfortably in place, glancing down her short road to the intersection. "Look, I need to get to work early so I can take care of paperwork. I'm…trying to work on something that will enable me to leave here for a while."

"Really?"

"Yeah."

"What is it?"

"I don't know if it will come together or not, so I don't want to say much."

Kevin's expression changed and he stared down at his breakfast and back at her. Shame flamed her cheeks.

"You can't go on like this, Kevin."

"No?"

"And your friends. How long are they going to be able to keep watching George?"

"As long as the funds hold."

Her eyes widened. "You mean, *you're* paying them? From your money?"

He shrugged. "The department's budget isn't what it used to be."

He tried to make a joke of it, and yet, knowing Kevin was paying for her protection out of his funds and time made matters worse.

Kevin pushed the truck door open and stepped out. As if reading her mind, he said, "Look, it's no big deal."

"It is to me. Money is not just something you throw around."

"I agree."

She swallowed hard. "I don't have the money to pay you back."

"I don't expect you to. It was my decision to do it. If I didn't want to do it, I wouldn't have."

She shook her head. "I don't understand. A few days ago you didn't even know me and now you're paying other police officers to do work on my behalf?"

"The way I was raised, you give help when it's needed. That is, if you can. We do this sort of thing in my church all the time."

"Your church?"

"Yes. When someone needs assistance, others step in and help. Sometimes it's financial. But sometimes it's giving time and a little sweat. Like when one of the women in our congregation lost her husband after a long illness last year, and needed her roof replaced. She couldn't afford to pay for supplies and labor, so some people pitched in for supplies, and a bunch of us got together, and over the course of the weekend we did the work for free. It helped her out."

"And you expected nothing for it?"

"I got the satisfaction of knowing I'd helped someone who wasn't going to be able to get the job done otherwise. I'm a firm believer that God works through each of us."

"Is that what you're doing for me?"

"You don't believe me?"

"I don't know what to believe."

It was clear from the way Kevin spoke about his church that he took his Christian faith seriously. While Daria had known other people with strong Christian values throughout her life, she'd never felt a desire to understand what made them faithful. Hearing Kevin talk about his faith and giving of himself made her curious, and eager to learn more.

"Maybe we can continue this discussion over dinner," he said.

"Dinner?"

"Yeah. It'd have to be here though. I don't want to risk having you out in public any more than you need to be. I'll bring some takeout with me after my shift. Do you like Chinese?"

"I'll cook," she finally said. "It'll be better than getting a sugar rush from muffins and cookies." And if things went well today, maybe there would be something for both of them to celebrate tonight.

He chuckled. "Sounds great."

Resisting the urge to place her hand over her rapidly beating heart, she forced a smile. It would do no good to let Kevin see just how much he had affected her. "Good. I'll be home around sixish."

As she was about to turn back to the house, Kevin stopped her with a light hand on her arm.

"I want you to think about something today."

She peered up at his serious expression. "What?"

"I was thinking last night that we may have to pull an Al Capone to get your ex-husband behind bars."

She chuckled, but then frowned in confusion. "Wait, an Al Capone? What's that?"

"You know, Al Capone wasn't taken down for boot-legging alcohol. He was convicted on tax evasion. I know George had some business with a loan shark, but there's nothing illegal we can pin on him. I want you to think about his dealings and tonight, you can tell me what you remember. Even if you think it's insignificant. It might lead us somewhere."

"I don't know anything about his business dealings. He never really talked about them because he knew I was sensitive about the money he spent."

"Just think about it."

She nodded, uncomfortable with the notion of having to revisit her relationship with her ex-husband yet again. She wanted that to be the past, but George clearly was making himself part of her present.

Daria walked the length of the driveway back to the house. After locking up and braving her exit through the back door, she climbed into her truck. Kevin was still sitting at the curb, his engine warmed and exhaust from his tailpipe making a cloud into the street.

She started her truck, then pulled out of the driveway carefully. When she got to the intersection, she glanced in the rearview mirror. Kevin had pulled his SUV behind her truck, put his signal lights on to indicate he was going in her direction.

She couldn't help the smile that tugged at her lips. He'd follow her to the office again, just as he had yesterday. And while yesterday it had annoyed her, today she felt differently. She wasn't going to pretend to understand exactly what those feelings were. She just knew that he made her feel safe.

She'd never met anyone quite like him. He gave willingly and without seeming to want anything as payment in return. It was about time she did her part and helped him in his quest to arrest George.

But more than anything, Daria was looking forward to their dinner tonight and exploring exactly what made Kevin the Christian and the man that he was today.

SEVEN

"**Y**ou look like roadkill."

Kevin looked up from the paperwork on his desk to Jake's amused face. "I think I am roadkill. I've been looking through Carlisle's file all morning and I can't find so much as a business card to connect him to anyone in Providence with illegal dealings. No phone calls. No business connections. Nothing."

"You're forgetting Milo Brickster."

Kevin glanced up at Jake. "No, I'm not. But except for the fact that Brickster is a purported loan shark that gave George Carlisle quite a sizable loan, we have no other direct connection."

"What about an associate of Brickster's? Someone at the salvage yard? Brickster is part owner of the salvage yard and Carlisle chose that spot for the meeting. Maybe they work through a middleman. Who's the other owner?"

"Paul Cross. His record is squeaky-clean. A few parking tickets and an old DUI from about twenty years ago. Nothing since."

"I wonder how he partnered up with Brickster."

Kevin flipped open the file on the salvage yard. "Seems like Brickster has been a partner from the beginning."

"That may or may not rule out strong-arming his way in if Cross needed money."

"That doesn't give us a connection to Carlisle."

"What about employees at the salvage yard? Have you checked any of those yet?"

"There's a long list. I've gotten through about half so far."

"Anyone raise any suspicions?"

"One name that I'm going to look into a little deeper. Again, no connection to Carlisle yet, but he is from Daria's neighborhood."

Jake raised an eyebrow. "Really?"

"Yeah, a few streets over. Has a long rap sheet, mostly drugs and disorderly conduct. Not exactly the type of guy you'd picture George Carlisle hooking up with. But then, neither is Brickster."

With his thumb and finger, Kevin rubbed the bridge of his nose. His eyes stung from looking through paperwork for the last few hours.

Jake laughed and pulled a chair closer to the desk and sat down. "You signed up for the gig."

"Yeah, I did. You don't have to remind me."

"Look, I'll help you out where I can. But no one would blame you if you pulled out of this. I mean, we're onto Carlisle. We've got him covered. It's only a matter of time until he trips up. And it's not like you haven't warned Daria Carlisle about what her husband is up to. You put it all out on the table for her. She made her decision to stay. There's nothing more you can do."

"I know you're right."

And Kevin did agree with everything Jake said. They were keeping a close watch on Carlisle. He had warned Daria of the danger she was in. Any other time that would have been enough. He would have continued to investigate and build a case against the perpetrator, and if the victim chose to stay and take the risk, well, then it was their call.

"So what's holding you back?"

"This is different. Everything about this is different than before."

"Including the woman?"

Kevin pierced Jake with a stare.

"Whoa!" Jake said, putting his hands up. "I'm just making an observation. I know where you're coming from. You've told me about your sister's friend, Lucy, and I've seen enough women like her over the years. You're always looking to rescue them from themselves. I'm just saying, you seem different with this one."

Kevin chuckled and rubbed his temples, fatigue getting the best of him. "She hates me being there, yet she brought me hot chocolate and an extra blanket last night. I think she really would leave if she could—she's an intelligent woman and she knows she's in danger— but she refuses to let it cow her."

"Not to mention she's pretty."

He glared at Jake, which earned him a laugh from his partner.

"But you hadn't noticed *that,* I guess."

The growing irritation that rose in Kevin was less from Jake's ribbing and more because his partner was dead-on right. Yeah, everything about this case *was* different. *Especially* the woman.

Daria was nothing like any other woman he'd known. And everything about her intrigued him, from her beautiful smile to her maddening stubbornness. But nothing had struck him as sharply as the loneliness he'd sensed from her that morning. She seemed truly surprised to hear that faith meant you didn't have to face the challenges of life alone.

Kevin knew he could count on the Lord for guidance and strength. And the members of his church community would be there in a heartbeat if someone needed help. His family no longer lived in Providence, but he couldn't imagine ever feeling as if he was truly alone.

Sure, Kevin had grown up a few blocks away from the church he still attended. He'd played in Little League with the guys in the congregation and even dated a few of the women who were now married and had families of their own. He knew all he had to do was say the word and half a dozen people would be at his door with help. That was the way he'd been raised, the way it was in his church community. But while he had a special sense of community in Providence, he knew that the faith that truly bound them meant he could never be separated from his spiritual community, no matter where he went.

Daria knew nothing of that. He wanted to be the one to teach her, to show her how God could heal that emptiness inside her that she'd tried to fill with her house. And maybe she could help him, as well, possibly turning out to be the answer to the problem he'd been talking over lately with God. The problem where he was ready to settle down, start a family, but couldn't seem to find the right woman to love.

Although he dated, there'd never been a woman who was special enough for Kevin to think about a permanent future. But he always believed that one day he'd find that special partner in his life. Someone to challenge him, give him comfort and raise a family of his own with. That person would have to have a strong relationship with God, as well. He simply couldn't imagine getting involved with a woman who didn't share his Christian faith.

Although curious about Christianity, Daria wasn't a believer. At least not now. And until she was, Kevin would ignore any feelings he had that were developing for her.

Jake slapped a file folder on the desk in front of Kevin, pulling him from his thoughts. "She must be some woman to have a hold on you like this," he said.

"What?"

"You disappeared on me in Daria Carlisle Land. I asked you what you knew about Marla Rickenberg's relationship with George Carlisle."

"Daria's assistant? As far as I know there isn't any connection to her ex. Why? What do you have?"

Jake shrugged. "Not much. Ski just called and said Carlisle was having lunch at Aluvia's with a woman who strangely resembles Marla. What do you think?"

A slow burn started in the pit of his stomach. Kevin looked at his partner. "I think Marla Rickenberg's having lunch with George Carlisle is a little too close for comfort."

Daria dropped her purse into the bottom drawer of her desk and fell hard into her desk chair. "That was a total waste of time," she said to herself. Rubbing her temples, she closed her eyes and willed the throbbing in her head to stop.

The little knock on the doorjamb had her looking up.

"Do you have a second?" Marla asked, holding Daria's coat in her hand.

Pulling herself together, Daria straightened up at her desk and motioned Marla to come in.

"You have my coat. Where did you find it?"

"You draped it over my desk when you stopped by to tell me you were leaving for lunch early."

"I thought I left it back at the bank."

Marla closed the door behind her, hung the coat up on the coatrack and then sat down. By the look on Marla's face, Daria knew this conversation wasn't going to be good.

"Please tell me you're not quitting," she said.

Marla rolled her eyes and chuckled nervously. "I can't even dream of quitting with the balances I have on my credit cards. No, it's nothing like that."

Daria drew in a deep breath of relief. "Good. Then what's up?"

Marla looked at her hands in her lap and nibbled on her bottom lip.

Daria laughed. "Come on. It can't be *that* bad. What is it?"

Marla hesitated a moment. "I had lunch with George today."

"George?" When Marla just looked at her as if she was afraid Daria would throw something at her, it clicked. "You mean you had lunch with my ex-husband?"

Marla nodded and then quickly added, "It was a spur-of-the-moment thing, but as soon as I got back, I started worrying. If it's going to bother you, I won't do it again. I mean, I know you're divorced and all and you said you were over him—"

"I am."

"But I don't want this to be a problem for us. I really like you and I'd hate to think I was doing something to hurt you. Does it bother you?"

Daria leaned back in the chair trying to get distance. Did she mind that Marla had lunch with her ex-husband? No. But she did question George's motives for seeking Marla out. And she did worry about Marla and what she could be stepping into, given what was currently going on.

"You're mad. I can tell. I'm so sorry."

"No, no." Daria waved off the comment. "It's not what you think."

"Then what is it?"

If Daria didn't choose her words carefully, she'd end up sounding like a jealous ex-spouse. Nothing was further from the truth. Marla was a nice girl and although Daria didn't always think the guys she went out with were "relationship material," her personal life was Marla's choice. Not hers.

But it was becoming increasingly clear that George Carlisle was steps beyond that. When she wasn't looking, her ex-husband had become a monster. Maybe he'd always been and she hadn't seen it. If that was the case, then Marla was an easy target, and Daria couldn't allow her assistant to walk out of her office without Marla's being a little on guard about his behavior.

"Did you call him or did he call you?"

Marla chuckled. "Does it matter?"

"Yes."

Appearing a little taken aback, Marla hesitated. "He called me and then he came to the office to pick me up after you left for lunch."

"I see."

"I should have asked you how you felt about it first, but I was afraid you'd be mad."

Daria shook her head. "Marla, you're a big girl. You don't need my approval to date someone. Even my ex-husband."

"But?"

"George isn't the person he seems."

With a drop of her shoulders, Marla said, "You *are* mad."

"No, really, I'm not. I just don't want you to fall for all that charm without knowing what's behind it. He can be very cunning."

Marla considered her words. "You were always so closemouthed about why you got divorced. Are those reasons what you're trying to warn me about?"

Those reasons seemed mightily irrelevant now. Back then George hadn't tried to hire a hit man to kill her.

Marla went on. "I mean, George always seems so sweet. Like he loved you so much. I'd love for a guy to look at me that way. What did he do? Have an affair or something?"

"Yes," Daria admitted.

Marla gasped softly. "Really?"

"Among other things. He likes to show off money. I'll bet he took you to some fancy restaurant."

"Aluvia's."

Daria chuckled, shaking her head. "That had to set him back some. Money he, no doubt, didn't have. You see, he likes people to think he has more than he does. He always finds a way to pay for it. But I never knew where that money came from, if you know what I mean."

It wasn't exactly true. At least some of the money had come from a loan shark named Milo Brickster. But did she really need to go into that much detail? Daria liked Marla. She also knew Marla liked to talk, which was why it had always been difficult to confide in her during her divorce. The last thing she needed was people in her office talking about her and her failed marriage at the watercooler.

"You mean, he's one of those sleazy guys who takes up with rich widows and steals their money right from under them without them realizing it?"

She could always count on Marla's imagination to run wild. This time Daria let her think what she wanted.

"I really don't know where he got all his money. But to get the kind of money he needed, he dealt with some business 'associates' that may not have been on the right side of the law. Even criminals have stock portfolios, and George meets a lot of people from all walks of life in his business. I didn't stick around long enough to find out what kind of 'business' they had with George."

"Wow," Marla said, nibbling on her thumbnail. "He doesn't seem like that at all."

"No." Admitting that left a sour taste in Daria's mouth. "Look, you can do whatever you want. I'm not angry about you having lunch with George. Really, I'm not. I just want you to be careful. Will you promise me you'll be careful?"

Marla nodded and quickly got up and left the office. Daria was relieved when she closed the door behind her. Normally, Daria liked her office door open so she could see the movement outside. She spent so much time alone at home that she liked the casual interaction when someone just popped in at her door to say hello.

But Daria didn't want the distraction. There was too much on her mind, not the least of which was her protector, Detective Kevin Gordon.

It amazed her how different Kevin was from her ex-husband. Just this one conversation with Marla put it all in perspective for her. They were opposite ends of a spectrum. It was hard to believe she'd been married to a man like George at all.

Where George had been all about impressing others with his money, Kevin used what he had unselfishly and didn't expect anything in return. He was using his own money and his precious time to keep her safe. What kind of man did that?

A man with a gentle heart. This was a man Daria wanted to know better.

Regardless of her feelings for Kevin, which she was having an increasingly difficult time ignoring, she needed to sort through her options.

But she had a lot of thinking to do now that her business at lunch had been a bust. It was on to plan B.

Kevin was sitting in his car as Daria pulled into the driveway a few hours later. A strange comfort, mixed with apprehension, washed over her. It surprised her how much seeing him lifted her mood after the disappointing day she'd had.

Reaching across the bench seat, she collected her lunch bag and purse before stepping out of the truck. As she turned toward Kevin's SUV, she saw him staring at her with the look of a man who'd been faced with a death sentence.

This can't be good.

"What happened?" she finally said, walking the few paces down the driveway to the curb. He hesitated before climbing out of his vehicle, slamming the door behind him.

He paused for a moment, as if what he was about to say would be uncomfortable for her to hear. "What is Marla Rickenberg's relationship with your ex?" he asked.

A strange burning coiled tight in her belly seemed to rise in degrees, squeezing the breath from her lungs. She really didn't want to talk about Marla and George.

"So you already know about Marla's lunch with George?"

A flash of surprise crossed his face. "Ski saw them at the restaurant together. The questions is why didn't you call me if you knew?"

"I *didn't* know, not until after the fact. And anyway, what would you have done? There was no crime in the two of them having lunch. Besides, I was busy." And she had been. Her longer-than-normal lunch meeting with the loans officer, coupled with her talk with Marla right afterward, had left work piling up on her desk. The granola bar she'd had this afternoon had done little to quell her hunger and now she was starving.

At his questioning stare, Daria added, "Marla and George have known each other in a casual sort of way through me for a couple of years."

"There was nothing casual about the way they were snuggling together in that corner table at Aluvia's during lunch today."

"Thankfully, she left that part out when I warned her about him."

"You warned her?"

"I had to. I couldn't just let her go off with George blindly. I didn't tell her about your meeting with him though."

"You mean, you didn't tell her he tried to hire me to kill you."

She looked around to see if anyone was listening. "No," she said quietly. "I just warned her that he's not what he seems."

"Why are you whispering? There's no one out on the street."

"Who knows who might be listening to us? I don't

want everyone to know every detail of what's going on. It's bad enough I have to know."

"Providence may not be small-town America, but neighbors have a way of finding things out whether you want them to or not."

"Terrific."

Daria glanced at the small scattered pile of garbage at the foot of her driveway where Kevin was standing. Now, that was the cherry on the cake of her bad day. In the next yard, Spot was barking. He must have had a feast in her can before the garbagemen had been by, leaving only this remnant of trash for her to deal with.

Grabbing the overturned metal garbage can, she walked to where Kevin was standing, plopped the can down and bent to pick up the trash. As if just noticing the debris on the ground, Kevin bent to help her pick up the mess.

"Let me do that," he said. "You'll get dirty."

"It's okay. I can wash up when I change. I do this every week."

"Are you always this stubborn when someone tries to help you?"

"I like to think of it as being independent," she said. Looking at the trash on the ground, she felt a little foolish arguing about accepting Kevin's help. But she'd always been independent. It had been an asset when she was married to George. He wasn't the type to coddle her too much. In his world, it was sink or swim.

"Did Marla say anything to you about the reason for lunch?"

Daria sighed. "Marla is an attractive woman. George likes to be noticed. It could be as simple as that." At least, she hoped that's all it was. It would make things so much easier if it were.

"You look like you're jealous." His voice was tight and his expression accusing, which irritated her.

"Hardly. I'm worried for Marla. Even after my warning today, I'm not sure she understands what she's getting into."

"She probably wouldn't listen anyway. But at least you gave it a try." Kevin dropped the last of the trash on the curb into her garbage can.

"Thank you for helping," she said, taking a cleansing breath.

"Believe it or not, it's not a sign of weakness to allow a man to be a gentleman."

His sudden, warm smile melted her irritation. "I'll have to remember that. I just wish Marla had told me about George before she went to lunch with him."

"Would that have made a difference?"

Daria thought about it a moment. "I don't know."

Marla's timing was more than awful. Daria had gone to work the day after Kevin told her about his meeting with George, intending to keep it a secret from her co-workers. She didn't really need anyone else hovering over her the way Kevin was doing, and she certainly didn't want anyone to feel as if they were in danger at the office. Now she questioned her decision to do so.

"He called her, not the other way around," she said, admitting the real reason for her worry.

"What are you getting at?"

"Marla met George at the Christmas party two years ago. And I think they talked at one of the company cookouts. George never seemed interested in her. He never talked about her, anyway. I've suspected for some time that Marla's been interested in pursuing a relationship with George now that he's a free man. But Marla said he was the one who'd called her, which makes me wonder why."

"I think it's obvious. He's toying with you. But he won't be a free man for long if I can help it, and Marla is not the target of his aggression, so you needn't worry."

Kevin spoke the words almost under his breath, but the bitter tone in which he said them didn't prevent Daria from hearing them.

Kevin cleared his throat. "I've been thinking. I'm not sure having dinner together is such a good idea."

"Why not? I thought you wanted to talk. And besides, I got a Christmas tree. I was hoping you'd help me decorate it."

He glanced over to the back of her truck, then propped his hands on his hips with a low chuckle. "You mean you were hoping I'd drag it in for you."

She snapped her fingers. "Busted. Actually, I hadn't thought about the dragging-in part until just now. Just decorating. But since you insist on being a gentleman, helping me get it inside is a bonus. Come on, what's the problem? It's only dinner," she said. "People eat. I know you certainly do. There's no sense our both eating alone if I have to cook anyway. I figured you could use a change of scene. Some holiday cheer. It's not like decorating a Christmas tree over a meal is a big deal that'll cause a scandal with the neighbors. You've been sitting on my curb for the last few days and giving Mrs. Parsons plenty to wonder about."

In truth, it was a big deal to Daria. She'd never been one to pursue a romantic relationship. With her nomadic lifestyle, it had been too difficult to start a romance, knowing it couldn't last. Friends, yes. The reality of having to make quick friendships, both male and female, had been there all her life, the way she'd grown up moving so often.

The pain of leaving a budding romance, only to have distance kill the relationship, had made her wary about taking risks where men were concerned. There were many times she wondered if that was the reason she'd jumped into marrying George. If they were married, she'd thought there would be no leaving. Boy, had she been wrong.

But something about Kevin had instantly put Daria at ease, and if nothing else, it was a friendship she wanted to pursue.

"I'll be honest with you. If things were different, if I'd never met up with your ex that night and I'd met you at the market like we did, I still would have noticed you." He drew in a deep sigh and shook his head just a fraction. "And I still would have accepted your invitation to come back here for coffee."

She smiled at his admission. Kevin looked directly at her. She liked that about him. He meant what he said and he wasn't afraid to say it. That kind of honesty was refreshing.

"Good. Then we don't have an issue here."

Kevin hesitated, gazing at her with eyes that grew darker, more intense as they penetrated her the way they did when he was all fired up. But he said nothing more. For either of them to move out of the cold and into the house, someone had to put an end to it.

Daria took one step toward him and cocked her head. "Look, it's starting to snow and my tree is going to get all wet and ruin my newly refinished hardwood floors. I don't make killer muffins, but I'm a decent cook and I could use the company while I string the popcorn for the tree. Despite everything that's going on, I actually enjoy your company. So if eating a meal with a friend is something that interests you, then great. We'll share a meal, have a little conversation over a root beer and then return to our regularly scheduled programming. If not, then you can get a sugar high on Mrs. Hildebrand's muffins and your trusty bag of Cheetos in your cold car. It's up to you."

As she stared at him, he smiled one of those killer smiles that always caught her off guard even when she was expecting it.

She didn't wait for him to say anything. Instead, Daria grabbed the garbage can and walked up the driveway toward the house. When she heard footsteps on the walkway behind her, she turned to find Kevin following her. A smile she couldn't hide crept into her cheeks.

"Independent, my foot. You were still going to make me carry the tree in, weren't you?"

She chuckled. "Yep. I may be independent but I'm not stupid. I'm wearing heels."

Daria hesitated at the bottom of the steps and waited for Kevin to lift the tree from the back of her truck and meet her on the porch.

"No dead birds tonight," she said with relief as she opened the screen door and pushed the key into the back-door lock.

"Is that why you wanted me to come?"

She flicked on the kitchen light and blinked at the brightness. "Sure. Plus, you know, carry the tree, kill the bugs, remove the mice and whatever else comes crawling into this old house."

"Women," he muttered with a chuckle.

"Hey, I heard that."

"I'm sure you did."

Dropping her purse and lunch bag on the kitchen table while Kevin shut the door behind him, she said, "Why don't you prop the tree against the window up front. I need to go to the attic and unearth what few Christmas decorations I own before we can start worrying about how to arrange it. In the meantime, make yourself comfortable in the living room while I get you a root beer. I have frosted mugs in the freezer."

He smiled kind of lopsided and tired and she felt her heart do this ridiculous acrobatic roll. She watched as he wrestled the tree she'd bought through the kitchen. It had been a spur-of-the-moment decision as she passed the Christmas-tree lot on her way home from work. The smell of pine filled the kitchen and soon would fill her house. She'd sweep up the pine needles that dropped to the floor later, when Kevin left. For now, she wanted to get dinner started.

It was only dinner and yet Daria was looking forward to spending time with Kevin tonight. No one had been to her house as a guest since she'd bought it. For the longest time it wasn't habitable, so company was out of the question. But there really hadn't been anyone she had wanted to invite until now.

She grabbed the frigid mugs from the freezer and dropped them onto the counter before pulling out a six-pack of her favorite bottled root beer. That's when the sobering thought hit her. She was actually excited about Kevin having dinner with her, yet she knew Kevin was here for a purpose. He was here to protect her, not because he wanted to spend time with her socially. She'd be wise to remember that.

"I can look upstairs for the tree stand and get it set

up while you're cooking. Or we could order a pizza or something if you'd rather work on the tree," he said, now standing at the kitchen doorway.

"I don't mind cooking. And it's really quick. Besides, you'll never find anything upstairs. There are tons of boxes." She handed him the mug of root beer. "You can take a load off while I get dinner ready. My coffee table is meant for putting your feet up."

He lifted an eyebrow. "I don't dare try that in my sister's house."

She laughed and added, "You look as if you're ready to drop on the floor. Go ahead. I'll be in the living room in a few minutes."

"I'd rather just talk to you."

She smiled as she busied herself in the kitchen with pots and food. "Okay. What do you want to know?"

"You mentioned you had something in the works today. How'd it go?"

"Oh." Her spirits immediately plummeted. "Well, I'd hoped to be celebrating the loan I was applying for. But it didn't go through. My credit is good, but I'm house poor right now and until that changes, I can't get an unsecured loan. I don't have enough equity in the house and you've seen my truck."

"I'm sorry it didn't work out. I appreciate that you're trying to find a solution to this situation."

"For both of us."

He offered her a weak smile. "Then my bank account thanks you, too. Have you given any thought to what I said this morning?"

"About George's dealings?"

He nodded.

She sighed. "I really haven't had much time. And

honestly, he didn't talk much about work. I found out about the loan shark quite by accident when someone in the building we were living in recognized him. George would have cut off his own tongue rather than confess it to me after I'd been hoarding pennies for so long. But he'd been acting strange, a mixture of being short with me and unusually sweet. So I knew something was up."

"Did he tell you how much money he owed or what it was for?"

"No, he said he didn't want me to get too involved in the whole thing, that he was protecting me."

"Protecting you? From what?"

"He wouldn't say. But I gave him what I had saved for the house and he used that. It was almost twenty thousand dollars at that point."

Kevin whistled in surprise.

"I know. I'd been saving for a while." She shrugged off the memory of turning over the money to her ex-husband. They'd been married. Of course what was hers was his. Even after all this time she had to fight to keep her anger over the whole thing from souring her mood.

"I'm going to be a few minutes in here," she said. "Why don't you take my mug and bring it into the living room and I'll be there in a few minutes."

"Okay," he said quietly. He took the mug from her hand and left the kitchen.

Daria closed her eyes, relishing the moment alone. Kevin was trying to help her put George behind bars and keep her safe. But she didn't want to have to relive the mistakes of her past to do it. She didn't want to talk about her marriage to George. She wanted to have a simple night where she didn't need to be afraid. She wanted to be happy in her own home again and enjoy the company of the man who made her smile.

Kevin had a smile that was warm and genuine and put her at ease. She should be terrified out of her mind after hearing the things George had said and done. But with Kevin, she wasn't.

She chose one of her tried-and-true recipes of sweet-and-sour chicken stir-fry over white rice not only because it was quick and she could prepare it without fail, but because it was the only thing she had all the ingredients for in her kitchen.

Glancing in the living room, she saw Kevin had taken her up on her suggestion about putting his feet up. The prospect of sitting on the sofa with Kevin, just talking for a while, was inviting. She wanted to know the man, not just the cop. She wanted to talk like normal people do, about normal insignificant things that had nothing to do with murder or danger.

Kevin wanted to talk about George. She'd meet him halfway. If there was something in her brain that he could use to put George behind bars and end this craziness, she'd have to find it. But she had no idea what that might be.

With dinner simmering, she wiped her hands with the dish towel and strode into the living room to grab her root beer.

She stopped short at the door.

Still clad in his black jacket, Kevin rested with his body reclined back and his head slightly tilted to one side. One foot was propped up on the coffee table, the other limply rested on the floor. His eyes were closed and his mouth was slightly parted. Relaxed in sleep as he was, Daria found it hard to tear her gaze from him.

He had to be dead on his feet. How could he possibly keep up the pace that he'd been maintaining these last few days? He looked so peaceful that Daria questioned whether she should even enter the room for fear she'd disturb him.

But she did. She couldn't help herself. Kevin had only been inside her home a few times. Each time for just a short while and each time under strained circumstances. Kicked back on her sofa, he looked as if he belonged here. Almost as much as she belonged here herself. She wanted to get closer, enjoy the sight fully.

Letting out a slow breath, she gently sat down on the sofa, keeping enough distance from Kevin so as not to disturb his sleep.

Guilt stabbed at her. It was her fault he was so exhausted. She thought the loan would help her get away for a little while, but that hadn't worked out. She'd have to find another way.

She looked at the tree propped against the window. This Christmas was her first of what she'd hoped would be many Christmases in this house. And regardless of whether or not George still meant her harm, it looked as though she would be spending Christmas here. Alone. She couldn't expect Kevin or any of the other police officers Kevin had counted on these last few days to give up their Christmas for her. And it was only a matter of time before Kevin's body and his bank account would give out on him. There had to be another way. She just had to find it.

EIGHT

The steady drone of a drill penetrated Kevin's mind like a piece of wood splintering apart. He opened his eyes to the shock of light blinding him from the wrought-iron lamp on the end table. Confusion made him dizzy until his eyes focused enough to register his whereabouts.

Shielding his eyes, he took in the room and remembered. He'd come into Daria's house for dinner. A quick glance out the window showed that it was dark outside and it was still snowing. Out the window, the light from the street lamp shone down on crystal flakes that were still falling heavily. They'd probably have a good amount of snow on the ground before tonight's storm was over.

One foot was propped up on the coffee table, the other on the floor. His mug of root beer rested on a white napkin next to the foot resting on the coffee table. The napkin was now saturated from dripping condensation. A large bowl of already strung popcorn garland lay next to it. Daria was nowhere to be seen.

Rubbing his face, Kevin realized he must have dozed off before dinner had even begun. There was no use beating himself up over it. He knew it was only a matter of time before his body gave out from running on practically no sleep. Although he'd worked many double shifts on cases before, and sat long hours on stakeouts, nothing had drained his energy quite as much as this case.

This one was different. There was no secret who the perpetrator was or the motive behind his actions. The only missing piece was evidence to nail him.

Kevin put in the hours at work, diligently combing through files, checking on leads that would give him even the smallest nugget of information about George Carlisle, anything that could help make an arrest against him for any crime stick. And while he kept his mind focused on his duty, there were visions of Daria meeting the same fate Lucy had.

He wouldn't let that happen. He'd do everything in his power to make sure Daria was safe from harm.

And he'd fallen asleep. *Good going, Gordon.*

He closed his eyes and offered up a prayer. Speaking softly he said, "Lord, I'm only one man. Obviously not nearly strong enough to carry this load alone." He continued his prayer to watch over Daria's home and for the Lord to give him wisdom and strength.

As Kevin finished, he thought of Daria smiling in the kitchen earlier when he brought in the Christmas tree. He couldn't deny there were feelings that went deep. Her smile played in his mind while he was sitting out in his SUV or when he was checking around the house in the early hours, just to give him something to do and keep himself warm.

A man's heart deviseth his way: but the Lord directeth his step. He needed direction on this one. The more contact he had with Daria, the more he was drawn to her.

As if his dreams had willed her back from wherever

she'd been, Daria appeared at the doorway. The sweat-shirt she was wearing had definitely seen better days. It must have been adorned with a college logo at one time or another, but constant wear and laundering had worn off most of the decal. In addition, paint stains were splattered down the front. The loose, faded blue jeans were just as well-worn and abused. The only thing that seemed untouched by paint were the white socks that were now slouched around her ankles.

"You're awake. I hope I didn't disturb you. I just thought I heard you talking when I turned off the drill."

She'd heard him in prayer. And by the warm look on her face, she'd heard his words. Kevin had never been shy about showing his faith. Yet he never pushed it on someone who wasn't open to receiving God's grace. Daria's curiosity was overwhelming and free of the judgment he sometimes saw in other nonbelievers. It gave him hope.

"I'm sorry I fell asleep on you. I hardly remember sitting back on the sofa before waking up."

"Despite the age and appearance, the sofa is comfort-able. I should know. I slept many nights on it before I was able to afford the bed."

"You don't have to let me off so easy."

The smile he'd seen when he woke up was now replaced with a frown. "You can't keep this up, you know. Even you have to see that."

Daria must have thrown an afghan over him while he slept. As Kevin lifted himself to a seated position, the blanket fell until it was half on the sofa and half on the floor. He picked it up, taking in the scent of it as it drifted to him. It smelled like Daria.

He made a tired attempt at folding the blanket, and

set it next to him. But it ended up looking like a crumpled ball.

"I'll be fine. I just needed a catnap."

Daria leaned against the doorjamb. "I kept dinner warm. I figured you'd wake up at some point and be famished."

He scrubbed his hand over his face. "What time is it?"

"Around ten-thirty or so. Maybe later."

"Wow. I didn't mean to sleep that long."

"I found the Christmas decorations upstairs. There's not nearly as much as I thought I had. So the tree will be a little bare. But I strung some popcorn, and Christmas-tree lights always make a tree look festive."

"You dressed like that for popcorn garland?"

She quickly glanced down at her sweatshirt and made a face. "I finished quick, then got a little sidetracked working on the bathroom."

Kevin looked at her quickly and blinked. "I can't believe I've been asleep for four hours."

"You were exhausted. I'll get your dinner." Daria scuffed her socked feet against the floor as she made her way to the kitchen.

Kevin started to follow on her heels and looked back at the tree propped up against the window.

"Why don't I get the Christmas tree set in the stand while you get that plate?"

He was starving. But he didn't want to eat his dinner while she watched. Getting the tree ready would give Daria the opportunity to decorate the tree while he ate.

Within a few minutes Kevin was on his knees tightening the last screw against the tree trunk. The smell of hot food had his stomach growling.

"It's crooked," Daria said, putting his dinner plate on the coffee table.

"I know," he said, climbing out from under the branches. "But the tree is crooked so if you try to straighten it, it'll be too heavy and off balance anyway. This is the best I can do to keep it standing."

"Oh. I wasn't paying too much attention to how straight it was. I just wanted a nice tall tree that was full."

Kevin brushed the pine needles from his shoulder. "You got that."

He pointed to the plate that seemed to be calling out to him. "Do you mind if I dig in while you decorate?"

"Knock yourself out. But you're not off the hook. I want you to help me when you're finished."

Daria felt giddy as she rummaged through the box of decorations. The room seemed to come alive again now that Kevin had woken up from his nap on the sofa. All the same, it was hard to keep from feeling guilty for wanting his company when he so clearly needed the rest.

Daria liked seeing him sleep, but liked even more when he was awake and she could gaze into his expressive eyes. She loved his eyes—their depth, crystal-blue color and the light that danced in them when he looked back at her. His hair was still tousled from sleep. Strands of gold and brown had fallen forward, giving him a rumpled look. The effect was completely adorable.

She'd been happy living alone in this house. Or so she'd thought until Kevin had shown up. In truth, she'd kept herself too busy to think about loneliness. It wasn't until she was sitting beside Kevin as he slept that she realized just how empty the house felt.

Shaking off the feeling enveloping her, she settled on

HOW TO VALIDATE YOUR
EDITOR'S FREE GIFTS!
"THANK YOU"

1 Peel off the FREE GIFTS SEAL from front cover. Place it in the space provided at right. This automatically entitles you to receive 2 free books and 2 exciting surprise gifts.

2 Send back this card and you'll get 2 Love Inspired® Suspense books. These books are worth over $10, but are yours absolutely FREE!

3 There's no catch. You're under no obligation to buy anything. We charge nothing — ZERO — for your first shipment. And you don't have to make any minimum number of purchases — not even one!

4 We call this line Love Inspired Suspense because every month you'll receive books that are filled with inspirational suspense. These tales of intrigue and romance feature Christian characters facing challenges to their faith and to their lives! You'll like the convenience of getting them delivered to your home well before they are in stores. And you'll love our discount prices, too!

5 We hope that after receiving your free books you'll want to remain a subscriber. But the choice is yours — to continue or cancel, any time at all! So why not take us up on our invitation, with no risk of any kind. You'll be glad you did!

6 And remember... just for validating your Editor's Free Gifts Offer, we'll send you 2 books and 2 gifts, *ABSOLUTELY FREE!*

YOURS FREE!
We'll send you two fabulous surprise gifts (worth about $10) absolutely FREE, simply for accepting our no-risk offer!

Steeple
Hill®

The Editor's "Thank You" Free Gifts Include:

- Two inspirational suspense books
- Two exciting surprise gifts

▼ DETACH AND MAIL CARD TODAY! ▼

YES!

PLACE
FREE GIFTS
SEAL
HERE

I have placed my Editor's "thank you" Free Gifts seal in the space provided above. Please send me the 2 FREE books and 2 FREE gifts for which I qualify. I understand that I am under no obligation to purchase anything further, as explained on the opposite page.

We want to make sure we offer you the best service suited to your needs. Please answer the following question:

About how many NEW paperback fiction books have you purchased in the past 3 months?

❏ 0-2 ❏ 3-6 ❏ 7 or more

123 IDL EZKP   323 IDL EZMD

FIRST NAME	LAST NAME

ADDRESS

APT.#	CITY

STATE/PROV.   ZIP/POSTAL CODE

FOR SHIPPING CONFIRMATION

EMAIL

PRINTED IN THE U.S.A.

(LISUS-EC-09R3)
© 2009 STEEPLE HILL BOOKS

The Reader Service — Here's How It Works:

the box of Christmas decorations she'd pulled out of the attic and began searching for the lights.

Without a word, Kevin sat down on the sofa and gave his attention to the dish she'd placed on the coffee table.

"Aren't you going to eat?"

"I ate earlier."

Funny how in the last six months she'd been alone here. But tonight, for the first time since she'd moved in, her house breathed with life. It felt like a real home.

"What made you decide to buy this beat-up old place anyway?"

She lifted an eyebrow in challenge. "Why? You don't like my house?"

Kevin chuckled, wiping his mouth with his napkin. "I can see I'm going to have to tread lightly on this subject. All I meant is there is a lot of work here for one person. And it looks like you're doing most of it yourself. That has to be hard."

"You don't think I can handle it?"

"I think you can handle pretty much anything you put your mind to. I just can't figure why you'd want to bother with all this work in such a big house. Why not a smaller house that was move-in ready?"

She looked at him wistfully as she set another wound-up strand of lights on the chair by the tree. Satisfied she'd found all the lights, she put the box down on the floor.

"There's something about getting your hands dirty, building your own space to call home. It may not look like much now, but it's shaping up to be a nice home. One day I hope it's filled with a lot of kids."

"You planning on having a husband with those kids?"

"That's the plan. But not for a while." She sighed,

pulling at the first string of lights to untangle it. "There's a lot I need to get through before that can happen."

He nodded his understanding. How could she even think of having a husband and family while George was after her? She hated the idea that her life was on hold this way, especially when she wanted to explore the possibility of something more with the man sitting in her living room right now.

Kevin seemed oblivious to her musing.

"At most I think I've lived in three different places my whole life," he said. "And the first one had no space at all. It was probably the size of your kitchen and living room total. When I was real young, I shared a room that was about the size of a broom closet with my older sister, Judy."

"You must have hated that."

He shrugged, watching as she struggled in vain to untangle what was a massive nest of Christmas-tree lights. "It wasn't so much sharing space as fighting for it. Between my sister's mountain of stuffed animals and her endless supply of perfume and girlie things, I barely had an inch of space to my name. I still don't know what half of that stuff was."

"We girls do tend to collect things."

In frustration, she gave up on the string of lights she'd been working on that refused to come untangled and picked up the next set, holding one end and bouncing them up and down in the hopes they'd fall loose.

"When Mom married my stepdad," Kevin continued, "we moved into a house in a neighborhood a lot like this one. I was about eleven then. It's actually not all that far from here."

"Really? Do your parents still live there?"

"No. They moved down south. Dad couldn't take the cold and he likes his fishing. He can do that year-round in Florida." He dropped his fork on the empty plate along with the crumpled napkin. "This was really good. Thanks."

Kevin started to get up with the plate still in his hand, but she waved him back.

"Leave it there. I'll get it later when I finish the rest of the dishes."

Kevin settled back on the sofa, rubbing his stomach as if he was satisfied.

Daria smiled. "Tell me more about your family."

"Dad married Mom when I was eleven. I wasn't too happy about it at the time. I figured I'd lived without a father my whole life to that point, why bother having one at all? But he raised me. He's the only father I know."

"You get along well with him?"

"Now I do. Not in the beginning, though," he said, reaching across the sofa to rummage through one of the boxes she'd taken down from upstairs. One by one he pulled her carefully packed ornaments out of the box and placed them on the coffee table as he talked. "Making us a family was a hard job for my mom. But she did it. I know it's stupid, but I sort of felt a little left out when Mom got remarried. But I think Dad knew that."

"What changed things?"

"Sailing," he said, a smile splitting his face. "Have you ever gone?"

Daria shook her head.

"Ah, that's too bad. You really should sometime. There's nothing like catching the wind and flying with it."

He stopped what he was doing only for a brief moment. His hands went up in the air as if he was mimicking his words and he was flying. Then he went back to his task.

"I remember one day a few months after we moved to the new house I was sitting in my new room with all this space, feeling pretty pitiful because I didn't know anyone in the neighborhood yet. I heard my stepdad pull into the driveway towing a small dinghy. Nothing special. Just an eleven-footer. They'd just bought the house and it was all he could afford. I'll never forget the look on his face though. It was if he'd just bought the *Queen Elizabeth II*.

"Mom was pretty ticked off he'd spent the money on the boat since she'd been eyeing some new furniture. Judy couldn't have cared less about taking a sail, but me, I just about jumped on the back of that thing. I would have ridden all the way to the boat ramp sitting in the back of the trailer if I could have."

Kevin laughed at the memory. "It was the first time me and my stepdad ever spent any real time together. Before that I was mostly afraid of him. He yelled a lot, had a short fuse where kids were concerned. He didn't have any kids of his own and then in one fell swoop, he got two."

"It must have frightened you when he yelled."

"A little at first. But I quickly learned how much he cared about us. He taught me a lot, mostly about God and faith."

She paused in her efforts to pull the lights free. "Your mom wasn't a Christian when they got married?"

"Not when they first met. Dad used to say that Mom was looking for something and needed direction. He just pointed her in the direction of the Lord. By the time they got married she'd become a Christian. It took a little longer for me though. I credit my stepdad for bringing me to the Lord at a time in my life when most kids think they know everything and need no one."

"Aside from weddings and funerals, I've never been to church. I wouldn't know what to expect. My parents never talked about God and faith."

Kevin glanced at Daria then. She sensed there was something he was about to say and then didn't. The silence that dragged between them was unsettling.

Noticing she was still struggling with that string of lights, he got up from the sofa and said, "Give me those things. You're making a mess of them."

"Gee, thanks. I thought I was doing okay."

She handed him the tangled mess she'd been working on and turned her attention to the box of ornaments. He'd already emptied one box on the table, so she opened the package of hooks and started connecting them to the ornaments.

"Do these work?" Kevin asked, finally getting them free.

"Last time I used them they did."

"How are your electrical outlets?"

"You're not going to get zapped when you plug them in, if that's what you're asking."

"Good."

With all the hooks connected to her ornaments, she went back to work on the lights as Kevin plugged the string into an extension cord.

"Do you mind my asking what you were praying about?" Seeing the surprised look on Kevin's face made her heart drop. "I just…when I walked in I heard you. I'm sorry. Is that something I shouldn't ask?"

His lips lifted into a slow smile. "You can ask me anything you want. I tell you what, though, why don't you come with me to church this Sunday? I think you'd really like the pastor. And maybe he can help answer some of those questions you have spinning in your head."

Did she want to go? She really didn't know what to expect. It had never been that she'd rejected the idea of God and faith. She'd just never taken a step toward getting to know more. Like Kevin's mother, maybe all she needed was direction.

"I don't know."

Kevin's eyes were warm when he looked at her. "It takes a first step to let God in. Just a step."

"Can I get back to you on that?"

"Sure."

Kevin reached behind the Christmas tree and plugged the extension cord into the wall. The lights immediately started to glow and twinkle. As she admired how they reflected in the window, doubling the glow, a movement outside caught Daria's attention. She took a quick step back, dropping her string of lights to the floor. The noise it made startled Kevin, who moved away from the window just in time before a large object flew through the glass and into the room.

Kevin grabbed her and instinctively pulled her away from the window. "Stay down," he ordered.

Peering out the window, he added, "Did you see who it was?"

Blood pumped through her and as she leaned to pick up the string of lights she'd dropped, her hands shook. "That's just it. I didn't see anything. It was a shadow. I thought I saw something moving outside. And then something came at the window and I reacted."

Kevin had already shrugged into his jacket and was headed toward the door. She followed him and placed her hand on his arm. "No, don't go."

"Why?"

He'd already changed from the carefree friend who'd been stringing her Christmas-tree lights, to the police officer who was there to protect her.

"I...just want you to stay."

He looked at her for a brief moment. "Stay away from the windows and don't touch anything. I'll be right back."

The front door opened and brought a gust of cold air into the foyer and then closed again, leaving her alone. Ignoring his request, she peered through the gaping hole in her window and watched Kevin walk around the snow-filled front yard.

The brick that had made the hole was now lying on the floor next to the coffee table. It was filled with snow and dirt, as if someone had dug it up from her front yard.

She couldn't sit still. She needed to do something. So she went to the kitchen and grabbed the broom and dustpan from the cabinet. She swept the floor, careful not to disturb the brick in case there was a way to get evidence off it. She didn't see any writing on the outside.

As she dropped the shards of glass into the garbage can in the kitchen, she decided she'd seen too many movies. It was probably the same kids who'd left that bird on her door coming back to get another thrill. They probably saw her and Kevin in the window and thought they'd get a good laugh for themselves.

It was expected to snow most of the night, leaving her with another mess to clean up in the morning in the way of snowfall. And if she was going to get to work on time, Daria was going to have to get up early anyway to shovel the driveway. It was nearly eleven o'clock already and chances were she wouldn't finish putting the tree together before it was time to turn in for the evening, even with her meager Christmas decorations.

Cold air was gusting through the window as she made an attempt at putting the lights on the tree while she waited for Kevin. But her nerves were shot. Someone had thrown a brick through her front window and left an angry hole in its place.

Daria finished stringing the last strand of lights and checked out the window again, wrapping her arms around herself to keep from shivering. She had a scrap piece of plywood in the basement to cover the hole, but it was going to be an ugly reminder of what had just happened.

She quickly ran to the basement to retrieve the plywood and then brought it to the living room. When she looked outside again she couldn't see Kevin out front.

The door opened and closed, jarring her.

"So?"

"There's so much snow that it's hard to see, but there are definitely tracks in the snow out front. I think they pulled a brick from your walkway to do the honors."

She pointed to the brick that still lay on the floor. "I figured as much. I brought up a piece of plywood to cover the hole."

Kevin was still standing by the doorway. "I'll help you get that plywood up on the window."

She waved him off and took a step toward him. "Nah, I can do it. I've nailed everything else into this house. What's one more board."

"Are you sure?"

"Yeah."

"Good. Will you be okay tonight?"

He was acting strange, not at all like he'd been earlier.

"You're here," she said. "Why wouldn't I be okay?"

Their gazes locked for a short moment. Daria wasn't a stupid woman. She knew the look of a man who was interested in more than just a casual way. She had to admit, the lines had somewhat blurred between them.

She watched the rise and fall of Kevin's chest beneath his jacket, saw his lips part ever so slightly as he took another step toward her. He was going to kiss her. She was sure of it.

But when he bent his head and she lifted her face to him, he surprised her yet again by kissing her on the forehead.

"Thank you for dinner. It was really good," he said quietly. "Good night, Daria."

Her eyes widened. "You mean you're leaving? Just like that?"

"Yeah. If you don't mind, I'm going to hang on to that blanket you gave me last night. It did a lot to help ward off the cold. It made last night bearable. I'm going to pull my SUV into your driveway, too, so the snowplows can get down the street easier, if that's okay."

"Sure. But I thought you wanted to talk."

Kevin already had his hand on the doorknob. "I did. But it's been a long day and I want to give Ski a call to see if your ex has settled in for the night. As soon as I know that, I'll feel better and maybe get a little more sleep in the car."

The door was half-open when she blurted out, "Stay the night in here. I…mean, I'd feel safer with you in here than outside. I know it sounds strange. I've been living alone here for six months. But…there's no reason to sleep in the car when I have a perfectly good sofa right in the living room. It's so cold outside. Surely there's nothing improper about you staying on the sofa. Unless you're afraid of another brick coming through my window."

He smiled at her lame attempt at a joke.

"Thanks for the offer. But the blanket will work just fine." He pulled the door open and a gust of wind and snow blew into the foyer.

"Did I do something wrong?"

When he was on the porch and out in the cold, Kevin turned. "No, I did. I actually forgot the reason I'm here. And that can't happen. Ever."

Daria groaned with frustration born from this complicated situation they were in and her own personal struggle. Tonight had not gone at all as she'd hoped.

"This is ridiculous. Me in here in this warm house and you out there in the cold. Is this what you really want, Kevin? To sleep in a cold car for the rest of your life just to keep me safe?"

Kevin was silent for a long time, his jaw tight as he kept his control. He lifted his hand and rested it on the doorjamb, moving in ever so closely until his face was just inches from hers. "I'm supposed to be protecting you, Daria. Keeping you safe from your psychotic ex-husband."

"So I'll lock the door," she argued. "You just said nothing is out there. I… If you were this tired tonight, I can't imagine how tired you'll be tomorrow and the next day. You can't keep this up. I don't understand why you just can't sleep on my sofa."

"Because it's best if I don't. And because to be honest, when I look at you in the lamplight like this, when your hair is slightly messed and you've chewed off most of the lipstick you wore today and you're wearing this incredibly ugly, paint-splattered sweatshirt that's five sizes too big, you look amazing. All I want to do is take you in my arms. And that can't happen."

Daria lifted her chin. "Why? Because you're supposed to be protecting me?"

"We're different people right now. In different places in our lives."

Confusion whirled around her. "What does that mean?"

"I'm a Christian. And I like you. I like you a lot. I love that you have all these questions about God and faith. But until we're in the same place, with the same beliefs, I—"

"Can't allow yourself to get involved with someone who is not Christian? That's why you didn't want to have dinner earlier?"

He sighed. "Yes, my faith is important to me. And you're becoming important to me. But it's more than my faith holding me back. Until that brick came flying through the window, I forgot my reason for being here. That's never happened to me before. I think it's best I keep my mind on my reasons for being here. For now."

She nodded without saying a word.

"Sweet dreams, Daria."

Kevin climbed off the porch and walked through the snow to his SUV without looking back. He had turned away from Daria, unable to deal with the disappointment he saw on her face.

He was genuinely attracted to Daria in a way he hadn't been attracted to a woman in a very long time. And he knew, with certainty, that she was attracted to him, as well. She'd wanted him to kiss her. And not on the forehead the way he had. That posed a problem he'd never found himself in.

The women he'd been involved with in his adult life were Christian women. Many belonged to the church he attended. And although Daria asked questions about his faith, she hadn't embraced the Lord in her life. At least not yet. That made it impossible for him to act on any of the feelings he had for her.

While talking about his faith, allowing her to see a relationship with Christ through him, was one thing, Daria herself would need to make a move toward her faith journey on her own. He couldn't force it on her. Until then, he wouldn't act on his feelings. He told himself it was for the best, especially considering her current situation.

Pulling his cell phone from his pocket he punched in Ski's number and waited as he watched Daria put the piece of plywood over the hole in the window. The noise of the hammer hitting the nail put him on edge just as badly as hearing the glass shatter around them in the living room.

It wasn't going to be a good night. With all the pent-up energy flying through him, Kevin doubted he'd get any more sleep.

As the cold bit into him as he walked toward the truck, he made a decision. There were a thousand reasons why he shouldn't be involved with Daria, not the least of which was her ex-husband's sinister plan to do her in. But he could be her friend. And if through that friendship Daria found the Lord, he would gladly see where it took them. Until then, he was outside in the cold.

NINE

Daria needed a little more than just a dab of makeup to hide the dark circles under her eyes this morning. It had been two days since the brick had come flying through her window. Two days of Kevin staying outside while she was stuck in the house.

Whether it was Kevin, Ski or Jake, someone was always there to escort her to work. And someone escorted her home, making sure she got into the house without incident and then watching the house from the outside. Kevin stayed the night in his car while Ski or Jake tailed George.

Kevin had made it clear he didn't want her wandering off during lunch, either. No errands to the bank or post office. If she needed groceries, someone would go with her. The brick had rattled him as much as it had her. The dead bird was bad enough. Now the vandalism was escalating.

She'd played their last evening together over in her head a hundred times in the past forty-eight hours. He didn't want to get involved with a woman who didn't share his faith. She understood that, to a degree.

It made her even more interested in learning why his

feelings for his faith were so strong. She wanted to know how that faith had shaped him into the man he'd become and how it had grounded him in his life.

He'd been forthcoming with answers to her questions, but he'd been holding back more than his emotions toward her. Even now when she tried to discuss it, he simply gave her a quick "sweet dreams" and headed to his SUV for the night.

Sweet dreams, my foot. She wasn't getting much sleep and she knew for sure Kevin couldn't be.

It had been snowing pretty hard when she came home from work last night. The snow had stopped sometime after midnight and the moon had come out full and bright. She'd spent much of the night watching the shadows the moon made dance across her wall as the night journeyed toward morning.

She got up early, ready to release all the excess energy she was feeling by shoveling the driveway. It was Saturday and she didn't have to go to work unless she wanted to put in some overtime. No, her time would be better spent getting work done on the house. She wondered what her guards would do. This was the first weekend since Kevin had appointed himself her protector. She knew he didn't think she was safe in the house without someone keeping an eye on her, but surely he had work to get to today. He couldn't just stay parked in front of her house for forty-eight hours straight.

She laced her boots and pulled on a warm knitted hat then wound a scarf around her neck. After she was done shoveling, she'd call to see if the new pane of glass she'd ordered for her window was ready to be picked up. Later she'd tear out the old plasterboard in the dining room and put a little extra oomph into it with the hammer.

She'd expected Kevin to avoid her as he had for the past two days when she headed out to clear the driveway, shovel in hand. To her utter amazement, he was shoveling her driveway. And he looked fabulous, refreshed, as if he'd slept a million years. Quite a contrast to his tense, exhausted appearance the last time she'd seen him close-up.

"Good morning," she said.

Reading the obvious surprise on her face, he said, "Jake stayed here last night. I was getting to that point where I felt semicomatose. The Trans-Siberian Orchestra could have been playing right next to my ear and I wouldn't have heard a thing. I wasn't going to be any good to anyone in the condition I was in."

"Jake was here? Not you?"

For all the restlessness she had gone through the past few nights, she hadn't realized there'd been a changing of the guards. Detective Santos had been at her curb and Kevin had gone home to his own bed and slept like a baby.

Daria fought the irrational irritation consuming her. He'd chosen to phone a friend and call in a favor to have someone else babysit her.

"Sleeping in my own bed last night did the trick. I feel like a new person."

"I'll bet," she said, looking away.

Kevin glanced at her clothing. "Work boots and jeans today? Looks like you're up for some physical work."

"I'm going to be working at home most of the day. You might as well get going yourself or you'll be late again."

He gave her a lopsided grin. "I like that you worry about me."

She didn't want him to be flattered. She wanted him

to be as irritated as she felt. But that was selfish. Brushing him off the way he'd brushed her off for the last couple of nights wasn't going to help the situation.

"You didn't have to shovel my driveway. I can do it myself."

"So you've said. I'm surprised you didn't sleep in on your day off."

"There's too much to do. And if I plan on leaving after New Year's, I want to get as much done as possible."

"You're leaving?"

She sighed. "Don't get excited. It's only for a few weeks. I get next year's vacation time January first. And I had a little bit of money put aside for some work on the house, so I thought I'd get away for a few weeks until the vacation money runs out. Your life can get back to normal. At least for a while."

He nodded and stabbed a snowbank with the shovel. "It'll give me some time to really dig and get some info on George. So what do you plan to work on today?"

Moving past him toward the truck, she said, "Don't you have to go into work today?"

"You're angry with me."

"Confused is more like it," she said, looking into his face, trying to find the emotions she'd seen the other night by the Christmas tree.

"I know. I know it's frustrating."

Daria drew in a deep breath. "Forget it. Aren't you going to be late for work or something? I mean, don't you have a life? Something that's missing you?"

"No, yes and no, unless you can count my house-plants, which have seen better days, too. But they're used to being deprived of nourishment. That's not what's really on your mind, though. I wanted to give you a little space about what happened the other night, but maybe we should talk about it."

"Okay. What's with you? First you want me to leave and then you look at me like you want me to stay and then you almost kiss me and then you don't. You tell me we're in different places. What does that mean? Is it because I'm not a Christian?"

"Yes," he admitted. "But it's more complicated than that."

She tapped the tip of the shovel she held in her hand. "Yeah, I get that. My ex-husband is a suspect in your case. He's trying to kill me and you want to catch him. I get all that." Daria threw up her hands in frustration. "You know, let's just forget about the other night. I have work to do."

Grabbing the shovel in a tight grip, she stalked back to the house until Kevin's voice halted her.

"I've taken some vacation leave, too," he called out.

She turned and looked at him. His face was drawn and he was clearly torn as much as she felt.

"Look, my falling asleep on you the other night, getting so wrapped up in this case the way I have, has shown me that I'm not a superhero. I know if you could get away from your ex you would and that would lessen the strain we're all feeling here. But until that happens we're left in a precarious situation. From now on until you're able to leave, I'll get some sleep during the day while you're at work. And Jake has agreed to take the lead on finding whatever he can dig up on George. When you're home, I'll be here. Maybe over the next couple of days we can figure some things out. Maybe find something we can use to get your ex-husband in jail. That has to be our focus for now. So I'm all yours today if you need help working on the house."

"You don't have to do this."

He blew out a frustrated breath. "You are the most stubborn woman I've ever met. Why do you have such a hard time accepting help from other people?"

Especially from you, she realized. Daria didn't want what he offered out of his sense of obligation. She wanted his friendship, his companionship and, yeah, she wanted more.

"I let you drag in the Christmas tree."

"Big deal!"

"I guess I'm just used to being on my own. Doing things myself. I'm not used to having someone—"

"To lean on?"

She shrugged. "Not even when I was married."

Leaving the shovel in the snowbank, Kevin walked over to her. "Well, you don't have to do it all alone. I wouldn't be here if I didn't want to be here."

Tears filled Daria's eyes. She didn't understand Kevin's hesitation. But she did feel his genuine friendship and concern and for those she was thankful.

"What do you know about hanging Sheetrock?" she finally said.

He gave her one of his high-voltage smiles that made her weak in the knees. "Enough to get the job done."

A few hours later, her first project of the day was done, and Daria was ready to move on to the next item on her checklist.

"You need a new vehicle, Daria." Kevin ran his hand alongside the truck and let his fingers test the spot of rust bubbling up over the wheel well. "This one has seen better days."

She'd had better days herself, but small talk about the

truck was good. It kept the focus off them and on something mundane. She could handle that. Needed it, even.

"Someday, but not for a while. It may not look like much but it's practical and dependable. The insurance is cheap. Just my price."

"While you're fixing up the house, I guess it's more practical than a car, too."

She smiled. "Exactly."

Kevin eased the tailgate down and then climbed up onto the bed of the truck. Daria handed him the snow shovel.

"The sun should dry out any residual snow and moisture on the way to the home-improvement store," he said as he pushed the snow off into the driveway. Daria used her shovel to pick up the piles of snow from the truck bed and toss them to the already high snowbanks.

"We only need a few sheets of Sheetrock. If the snow doesn't melt we can put down a tarp to keep the Sheetrock dry until we get it in the house."

They'd worked all morning pulling the decrepit plaster off the dining room wall. It had been an eyesore that Daria had had enough of. If they could get the new wallboard up today, she could mud and sand the wall tonight.

She grabbed the shovel from Kevin and watched as he jumped to the driveway and slammed the tailgate into place. When it locked, he pulled at it to make sure it was secure.

Daria couldn't help but feel melancholy looking back at the house. All this work she was doing and she might not even get to stay here.

"What's wrong?"

"Ah, nothing. I just need to remember to get another lock for the front door. I called, and the home-improve-

ment store has a windowpane-repair kit, too. Remind
me to pick one up?"

"Sure."

As she climbed into the truck, she decided having
Kevin here to help her was a blessing. Daria had
wondered how she was going to struggle with a 4 x 8
slab of Sheetrock all by herself and then lift it into place
without any equipment. As long as Kevin was her
shadow, he could be a huge help to her.

Kevin walked over to the driver's side. "Scoot over."

"It's my truck."

"I've seen the way you drive this thing," he teased.

She should have been offended, but she just laughed
and moved to the passenger's seat while Kevin climbed
in and took the wheel. They'd worked well together
today and she liked having him along for the company.

When she was a kid, she'd always hated feeling this
happy because it was a sure sign it was time to move
on. Her parents had the uncanny ability to stay in one
place only until she felt comfortable and started to make
friends. Then they'd announce plans to move.

It was a childhood fear that had stretched into her
adult life. But this time, it was Kevin who couldn't stay.
He'd be glued to her side until George was arrested, but
then he'd have to get back to his regular life. She only
wondered how long she'd be able to enjoy this time with
Kevin before something forced her or him to leave.

They spent little more than an hour at the home-
improvement store. It would have taken Daria twice as
long if Kevin hadn't been there to help her lug the
awkward sections of Sheetrock onto the dolly, then
maneuver it through the store and out to the truck. He'd

barely needed any help from her to lift each sheet and slide them into the truck's bed.

"Hello, Daria," she heard from behind. The familiar voice had been comforting at one time. But now, hearing George's voice struck fear in her and made her knees grow weak.

She swung around quickly, but Kevin had already straightened and stood in front of her like an armored tank. His expression was lethal.

"What are you doing here, Carlisle?" Kevin asked.

George ignored Kevin and kept his gaze on Daria.

"You're still fixing up that old relic, I see. Living your dream," he said, smiling.

Daria had never really noticed it before, but George's smile was anything but sincere. His tone was bright and cheerful, his posture relaxed, but everything else screamed that he was putting her down, looking down at her. He'd never shared her dream of finding an old house and making it their home. He'd placated her, telling her one day they'd have a house instead of the luxury apartment that was too expensive. But each and every time she'd scour the newspaper or drive street to street in search of something affordable, he'd always put her off.

She sighed. There were no regrets. Their dreams were different. It was a simple sign that she'd ignored that they weren't meant to be a couple. His infidelity was just one more reason. Well, no matter. She'd rectified that mistake by divorcing George. She'd moved on with her life.

"We have to go," she said and turned toward the door of the truck. Kevin remained like a rock wall in front of George.

She opened the truck door but stood outside, waiting for Kevin.

"There's no need to feel awkward, sweetheart," George said, looking past Kevin. "Did you know we were married for five years?" he said, finally looking at him.

She glanced at Kevin and saw he hadn't budged. He was like a formidable statue, stone cold and unmovable.

George lifted his shoulder, his hands hidden deep in the pockets of his tweed coat. "So, what are you two? An item?"

"What's it to you?" Kevin retorted. "You're divorced, remember?"

"How could I forget? But what is *your* role here?" George's eyes became ice. It was something Daria had never seen before and it turned her cold as fear crawled under her skin.

"I'm her bodyguard," Kevin said.

George's laugh was like nails against slate, grating on every nerve ending in her body.

"That's an interesting way to put it. I wouldn't count too much on his abilities, Daria. As I understand it, his reputation is under scrutiny. You wouldn't want a guard who gets so close that he can't see danger coming."

Eyes widening, Daria said, "What are you talking about?"

"Get in the truck, Daria," Kevin said through clenched teeth. "We're done here."

She stared at the two men, a war raging inside her. Then, her insides shaking, Daria climbed into the truck and locked the door. Kevin didn't need her protection against George. And George? She needed to be as far away from him as she could get. He wanted to kill her. She could see it in his eyes even as he smiled at her.

How could this be the man she'd married? How did she not know this side of him?

A few seconds later Kevin climbed into the truck, as well. George walked away toward the back of the parking lot.

"What did he say?"

Kevin glared in George's direction. "He gave me a line about donating blood."

She glanced across the parking lot to the blood-drive mobile. George was walking in that direction.

"It might not be a line. Ever since I've known George he's donated blood regularly."

"Right. I remember you telling me that before. He's afraid of tainted blood."

Daria nodded. "He's scared of germs and catching something from someone else. So every few months he goes to donate blood and have it frozen in case he ever needs it."

"Interesting. If he's that much of a fanatic about germs, I'm surprised he's risking a donation at a blood-mobile in a parking lot instead of at a sterile hospital."

"I'm finding out that George is full of surprises." Daria watched George's movement in her rearview mirror. "What did he mean about you being under scrutiny?"

"He's playing with me."

"Kevin, how could he have known…"

"That I was in your house when the window was broken?" Kevin shook his head. "I don't know. Ski was watching him. Carlisle was home the other night and never even went for his walk. The night guard verified it."

"Maybe it was just a figure of speech."

"Maybe."

Daria's blood turned cold. "Do you think George will follow us?"

Kevin took his eyes off the road for a brief moment and looked at her. The ferocious look on his face told her that for George's sake, the answer had better be no.

TEN

Daria wanted to cry. A bomb had gone off in her backyard. At least, it looked that way.

They'd been gone only a few hours, but the damage that had been done was extensive. The previously white blanket of snow that had made her house and yard look like a Christmas card now looked ugly and dirty, mixed with dirt around the yard.

The tulip bulbs she'd spent hours selecting and then planting last fall had been uprooted. Daria's spirits plummeted even further as she stepped out of her truck. Her mood hadn't even had a chance to level itself off after seeing George at the home-improvement store. Now this.

Spot was barking like a rabid animal in the next yard. If not for the fact that the snow shovels were strewn about in the backyard next to the dug-up flower beds, Daria would think the dog had broken free from his chain and had a field day digging yet another huge hole in her flower bed, as he had during the fall.

"Who would do this? Why would they do this?" she said, mostly under her breath. Tears filled her eyes and her bottom lip trembled as she eyed the destruction of all her hard work. She clamped her teeth over her lip before Kevin came up beside her.

"Let's get you into the house. Then I'll check with the neighbor across the street to see if they saw anyone," Kevin said. "If we get some witnesses to the vandalism I can file a report."

"What good is a report going to do? They keep coming back here."

The tension that had plagued Kevin throughout the ride back from the home-improvement store had now changed to worry. Pushing a lock of hair out of her face, Daria grimaced at the sight in front of her.

"My every attempt to beautify my yard seems to have been a waste of time."

Daria could only stand and stare at the destruction until she felt Kevin's gentle hand on her arm.

"Let me check the house first and then I'll go see if the neighbors saw anything."

Stumbling up the back-porch stairs, she slipped the key into the dead bolt on the back door. Try as she might, though, it wouldn't budge.

Irritation bubbled up inside her and she groaned. "This is odd. It's usually the front door that gives me trouble, not the back door."

Frustrated and feeling utterly defeated, she jiggled the key in the lock, tears blurring her vision.

"Let me try."

Kevin reached around her, but she swatted his hand away. Not only did she not want him to see her tears, she was determined to get the door open on her own.

"Put a little more pressure on it."

"I'll break the key in the lock if I force it any more."

"I might be able to get it to turn."

Giving in to defeat, she allowed Kevin to step in front of her and try the lock.

Kevin inspected the lock and began to jiggle the key.

"Have there always been scrapings around the keyhole?" he asked.

"What scrapings?"

Before Daria could see what he was talking about, the key turned.

"There," Kevin said with a grunt.

Opening the door and swinging it wide, Daria breezed by Kevin and walked into the kitchen first. As soon as she did, she stopped short and charged back, colliding with his chest.

Her body grew cold.

Kevin wrapped his arm around her as she fell against his chest, trembling violently. The quiet sobs that escaped from her lips made it difficult to speak.

"What is it?"

Holding Daria with one arm, Kevin pushed into the kitchen and immediately froze. She glanced back over her shoulder to see if what she'd seen was really there.

In a large heap on the floor was the hummingbird vine Daria had pointed out to Kevin that first morning. It sat on top of a large pile of dirt in the middle of the kitchen floor among the bulbs she'd planted last fall. It all looked ominous. The flowers George had given her, decayed from having been tossed in the compost pile for days, were arranged in a vase on the counter.

"Daria, I want you to get in my truck, lock the doors and stay there."

"No," she said on a sob.

"Get in the truck," Kevin said, his voice low but stern. "They may still be in the house."

Staring at the floor, she said, "And if they come running outside, I won't be safe there, either. The only place where I'm safe is with you."

Kevin didn't seem happy with her answer, but he didn't argue. Instead, he listened for obvious signs the intruders were still on the premises. Daria didn't hear any movement, but that didn't mean a thing.

Daria closed her eyes and hugged her middle as Kevin walked into the living room, gun drawn. She stood in the center of her kitchen, looking at the dirt on the floor from the pulled-up tulips as tears burned her eyes.

A stranger had been in her house and had breached that little sense of safety she felt. Even with Kevin sitting out front for days, someone had still had the nerve to break in and... Where did Kevin go?

Daria ran a few steps down the hall and immediately realized she should have stayed in the kitchen. In the living room, she was greeted by the sight of the Christmas tree knocked over on its side on top of more dirt. The lights were hanging off the branches and the popcorn garland she'd painstakingly strung was half on the tree and half on the dirt pile.

Unable to look at it, Daria turned and stalked past Kevin toward the stairway.

"Where are you going?" Kevin asked.

"I'll be right back." And she disappeared into the darkness.

"Wait, I haven't checked upstairs." But she was already gone.

Kevin fumed as he raced up the stairs after Daria. Somehow, with all the precautions they'd taken, George had still managed to touch her. And while this mess looked like random street-kid vandalism, the flowers in the vase screamed personal. George may not have used his own hands, but he'd definitely found a way to reach in, grab Daria and scare the daylights out of her. The question was, why? After everything he'd done to hide the fact that he was trying to get at Daria, why would he broadcast it like this?

"Watch out for the eighth step. It's very weak. I haven't had a chance to fix it yet," he heard Daria yell down as his boots hit the worn wood.

The wood groaned beneath his foot. He felt a slight bend, and Kevin figured he'd found what she was hollering about. Searching the darkness, he grazed the wall until he found the light switch. When he flicked it on, the room remained dark. The only light in the room was what was coming in from downstairs.

"There isn't any power up here," she called out. "There was a bad leak in the roof and it did a lot of damage in one of the rooms. The roof is fixed, but some of the electrical wiring needs to be replaced, so I had an electrician shut off the upstairs power for now."

A small beam of light came on in the last room down at the end of the hall. Kevin found Daria on the floor among some scattered boxes holding a large battery-powered emergency flashlight and poring over a large opened box.

"The only things of importance I have I keep up here because I don't want them to get ruined while I work. These don't look like they've been touched," she said, sniffing and wiping her wet cheeks with a quick swipe of her hand.

Kevin glanced around the room, walked over to the closet and opened it.

"I already checked it. There's no one up here."

"You should have waited for me," he said.

He heard her big sigh of relief. "Thank goodness, it's still here."

"What?"

"My great-grandmother's bracelet. It's the only thing I own, besides the house, that is of any real value. It's not worth a lot of money, maybe a few hundred dollars, but it's been in my family for a long time. It was the one thing my parents always let me keep when we moved. I would have been heartbroken if it had been taken."

"We need to check the rest of the house," he said. "Why don't you pack all that away and come downstairs."

"I will in a sec."

Kevin smiled, shaking his head as he turned away and walked to the doorway. *Stubborn woman.* He waited for Daria by the door. There was no way he was going to leave her alone until he knew where and how the vandal had gotten into the house.

They both went downstairs and he called the station as Daria looked around. He figured they could leave the bedroom for last, although in reality that was where thieves did the most damage. Most of a person's valuable possessions were kept in the bedroom in "secret" places under the mattress or in a hidden drawer.

One thing was for sure, finding evidence that a thief had rummaged through your most personal belongings was never easy, regardless of whether or not something was taken. It robbed a person of something much more valuable than money. It took away their sense of security. And Kevin knew Daria had already been struggling to hold on to hers.

* * *

By the time Jake arrived, Daria had confirmed that nothing on the main floor appeared disturbed except for the uprooted flowers in the kitchen and the overturned Christmas tree in the living room.

"It doesn't look like there was any forced entry on the main floor," Kevin said. "Although they definitely tried the back door. There are markings all over the lock. That's why you had a hard time with the key. They probably damaged the lock."

Jake pulled out a small brush and bottle of powder from the fingerprint-dusting kit. "What about the basement?" he asked.

"The bulkhead is wooden," Daria answered. "I haven't had a chance to replace that with a metal one yet. The wood may have been weaker than I realized."

"That may be how they got in."

Daria followed Kevin and Jake down to the basement, staying one step behind. Even though the small light at the base of the stairs was lit, Jake panned the musty cellar with the flashlight, delving into dark corners. Except for Daria's tools and an old table saw, the cellar was virtually empty. A short flight of stairs led to the closed bulkhead in the back of the basement.

Jake walked to the bulkhead and shone the light on the stairs. A long split in the wood by the frame said it all.

"That's how he got in," he said. But Daria wasn't paying attention. Instead, she was on the floor by the pile of tools, picking them up and putting them into their rightful place.

Kevin held her hand back. "Don't touch them yet. Don't touch anything."

Daria groaned, leaning back on her heels. "They took my big wrench. I can't tell you how many times that thing saved me from having a flooded basement before the plumbers did their repairs."

"Is the wrench all that is missing?"

She looked around. "I think so. They made a mess of my toolbox. These tools cost a small fortune and are too valuable with the work I'm doing in the house for me to just keep them on the ground like that."

Jake moved away from the door and shone a light in the direction of the strewn-about tools. "Any chance you could have left the missing wrench somewhere else in the house when you were working?"

Daria glanced up at him, lifting an eyebrow in challenge.

With a chuckle, Jake said, "Guess not." He snapped off the flashlight. "Is Ski tailing Carlisle today?"

Kevin shook his head. "Ski had to work with his dad today. You were on duty, so there wasn't anyone else to tail him since the department won't foot the bill. We didn't have to worry about what George was up to though. He found us at the home-improvement store."

"Any incident?"

"Other than sending my blood pressure through the roof, no. He made some veiled threats but nothing concrete enough to take action."

"So this couldn't be his handiwork."

"Not directly, anyway. Maybe he wanted us to see him at the home-improvement store to give him an alibi at the exact time he had someone here."

Jake made a face. "That's speculation. We can't prove that Carlisle had anything to do with this at all."

Daria had been quiet until now. "Why would kids put those flowers he gave me in a vase? They'd have left them on the compost pile."

That thought nagged at Kevin. But everything about this break-in screamed amateur.

"What are you thinking?" Daria asked.

Kevin sighed. They'd dust the tools. See if they could lift a print or two off one of them they could use to find out just who was involved. If they managed to make a match, they'd question the kids, see if Carlisle hired them to do the deed.

"Any pro who's been around knows what's valuable. Professional thieves know a gold bracelet like the one you have upstairs is easy to trace at a pawnshop. It's unique. Not to say they wouldn't take it if that was all they found. But if they came in through that bulkhead like we think, they would have hit pay dirt right here. You have a gold mine in this basement."

"What do you mean?"

"Tools, the good stuff like you have here, can't be traced and they gain high money on the open market. If whoever broke into the house knew what he was doing," Kevin said, pointing to the back of the cellar, "he'd have stopped right here, took what he could carry and left without ever making it upstairs. There wouldn't have been any need to go farther."

"What about the mess in the kitchen?"

"That's the point," Jake said. "Whoever did this was probably an amateur. The temptation of what you have here would have been too great for a professional thief. But nothing was taken. Whoever did this came here with a purpose. Not to steal from you. Maybe it was kids trying to have fun. Maybe it was something else. Regardless, I'm going to get started on those fingerprints."

When Jake went upstairs, Daria sighed, brushing her

hands on the thighs of her jeans. "I'd better go clean upstairs before the whole house smells like compost."

Kevin couldn't take it anymore. "Hold on a sec."

Taking two steps toward her, he gathered Daria into his arms. He'd wanted to give her space. But he couldn't bear to just stand there while she looked so hurt.

"You don't have to hold it all in," he said. "It's perfectly natural to have a good cry."

"I already did that upstairs."

"I don't mean a few tears. I mean, a good cry. You know, the kind where you just let someone else take care of you for a little bit while you have a meltdown? You hold so much in and take it all on your own shoulders, but you don't have to."

Daria sniffed. "I'm afraid if I start I won't stop. I'm scared."

They'd been face-to-face with George Carlisle earlier in the parking lot, but Daria's ex-husband had still managed to get too close to Daria in her house, despite Kevin's attempts to keep her safe. And he knew without a doubt George had a hand in this even if he couldn't prove it.

Lord, how has it come to this? Despite my every attempt to keep Daria safe, George still manages to get to her. I need Your guidance and clarity so I can keep Daria from harm.

"Make sure you say a few words for me," Daria said quietly.

And it dawned on him that he'd been praying out loud. His heart swelled with the knowledge that Daria was opening up to prayer. "Why don't you say a few words to express your feelings? He'll hear you."

"I don't know how." She shook her head slightly, a trace of embarrassment crossing her face. That was the last thing he wanted her to feel. She had nothing to feel ashamed about.

"Then come with me to church tomorrow and we'll do it together."

Daria nodded, her hands trembling. "Someone was in my house, Kevin."

The slight hitch in her voice broke his heart. To have your personal space invaded, the place where you feel safe and protected is a breach that isn't easily overcome.

"I know."

She glanced at him and swiped her wet cheeks quickly.

"Why does this keep happening? You're with me all the time. If not you, then Ski or Jake."

"That's the problem. Someone is always with you and yet you're still a target."

Tears were back in her eyes when she looked up at him. "I admit I'm becoming paranoid, especially about the flowers. But what if it really was just these neighborhood kids? They've been a nuisance for a long time and the police haven't been able to stop them."

"Smashing street and porch lights, even the bird, gruesome as it was, is typical of neighborhood kids who have a little too much time on their hands. But to keep coming back? Then escalating to breaking and entering? Seems too brazen to me, giving street hoods too much credit."

As the fury bubbled up his throat, choking him, Kevin realized things had gotten way too personal with Daria. He wasn't being a cop detached from the situation and looking at the facts rationally anymore. He'd lost his reason where Daria was concerned.

He pinched the bridge of his nose. The smell of wet earth and decaying matter filtered down from the kitchen and mixed with the scent of the musty basement. The sound of feet walking across the floor seemed to boom above them.

"I don't know why this keeps happening. And only to you," he finally said.

His arms tight by his side, he recalled the mess in the kitchen and the overturned Christmas tree in the living room. Daria's face still held the same shocked and fearful expression she had when she'd first come into the house.

Someone had been here, poking around, touching things that meant something to Daria. The next time it could be worse. They might actually reach her.

Kevin couldn't stand it. Closing his eyes to the image that tumbled onto him like an avalanche, he followed Daria upstairs and prayed Jake would be able to lift some kind of print that would eventually lead to Carlisle's arrest. He wasn't about to let Daria's ex get any closer than he had today. And one thing was certain. He wasn't going to leave Daria's side until Carlisle was locked up behind bars for good.

ELEVEN

The rest of the day went to cleaning up the mess. Kevin had refused to leave Daria's house, even to go home and change clothes. Jake brought over a fresh set of clothes that evening. He sat with her and made small talk over coffee while Kevin showered and changed, and every evening Kevin would sleep in his SUV.

The next morning, Sunday, she got up early, intending to meet the day head-on. She'd just finished putting on a dress when she heard a commotion outside her front door.

"What's all this?" Daria stared at Ski and the truck that had just pulled into her driveway. An older gentleman climbed out, opened a side compartment and began pulling gear out of the truck.

Ski waved to her from the other side of the truck. "Your new alarm system."

Daria looked at Ski, puzzled, and stepped out onto the front porch. "I'm not getting an alarm system."

That's when she saw Kevin, grabbing some of the gear the older man had put on the ground in the driveway.

"Did you have something to do with this?" she called out to him.

"That's right. Mr. Stanasloski is going to install a system that will make sure no one gets into the house without us knowing it." Kevin flashed a smile. "Hey, you look nice for a Sunday morning. I'm used to you in business clothes or sweats and paint-splattered shirts."

She'd gotten dressed up. Nothing fancy, but she'd chosen a pretty dress she seldom wore because she had no occasion to do so. She'd thought long and hard about her motives for wanting to go with Kevin to church this morning and decided it was something she wanted to do for herself, not just because she wanted to be with Kevin or just get out of the house.

The older gentleman walked up the path and stuck out his hand to shake Daria's. "I don't usually work on Sunday, but Ski said it was an emergency. Don't you worry though. No one is going to be able to so much as walk up to the front door without having a record of it on tape."

"But I didn't order an alarm system. And I can't afford one," she said as the men breezed by her into the foyer with all their gear. Ski followed and so did Kevin. She walked back into the house behind them.

Even with the two of them standing in the foyer alone, Kevin's voice was low. "Don't worry about that."

"It's my house. Of course I'm going to worry about it. You can't just install an alarm system without my consent."

Kevin dropped the roll of wires he'd been holding to the floor and took Daria by the arm. "Come with me a second."

She followed him into the kitchen, all the while watching Ski and his dad in the living room, unloading gear on the hardwood floors and strapping on their tool belts.

When they were alone in the kitchen, she said, "Kevin, you know I can't afford an alarm system. If I had the money for something that extravagant, then I'd be able to afford leaving here for a while."

"I know that," he said. "But after the last break-in it's clear that it's not enough for me to make sure you're safe when you're here. It's also important that we keep people from coming in when you're not home. Since neither one of us can be here all the time, it poses a problem."

She crossed her arms across her chest. "Yes, but what does that have to do with an alarm system?"

"I think we're in agreement that I can't watch you every moment of the day and night."

She nodded her agreement.

"And I can't afford to keep hiring Jake and Ski to do it when I can't because the department doesn't have the extra funds. I figure this is the best way to protect you without having a permanent bodyguard on you 24/7. And an alarm will cut down the likelihood that you'll come home to another break-in."

"An alarm system costs thousands of dollars that I just don't have now. I can't afford it."

"Think of it this way—you can't afford not to get it. The house will be under surveillance even when you're not here. That seems to be when these incidents are happening. The rest of the time, when you're going to work or coming home, I'll be watching. Besides, Ski's dad is giving you a sweet deal. He's hooking up the system for only the cost of parts as a favor to Ski."

"And to you?"

Kevin shrugged. "And me. He's a good guy. He's good at what he does. He's been installing alarms his whole adult life."

She sighed. "What'll it cost?"

"If you cut out stopping for coffee every day on your way to work, even you'll be able to afford the monthly payment plan he's set up. I'll cover the monthly monitoring fees. They're a lot cheaper than paying Jake and Ski."

Having overheard the conversation, Mr. Stanasloski came into the kitchen and stood at the doorway. "It's a good system, ma'am, and I'm happy to do this for you. It covers all the doors and windows. We even have security cameras that will monitor the grounds if you hear something and want to check things outside. It'll keep you safe."

"You have cameras?" she said. "I don't know that I like the idea of strangers looking at me."

Ski came in behind his dad. "Only you'll see what's on the cameras," he said. "It'll get recorded on loop tape that can be erased every day if there's nothing on it. The cameras allow you to see what's outside so you don't have to go and look for yourself. If the right code isn't punched in within twenty seconds of an entering on any window or door, a siren sounds that'll wake the dead. When that happens the police will be here in a matter of minutes."

Daria sighed. "My neighbors will love this."

Mr. Stanasloski added, "Your neighbors will feel safer. I installed one of these just up the street a few weeks ago, so you don't have to feel like you're the only one needing protection. A lot of people want that extra security. I've been doing alarms for over thirty years now. It's a good system and it'll help you sleep easy at night."

"Do I have a choice?"

Kevin pushed a lock of hair away from her face and

rested his hand on her shoulder. "Sure you do. It's your house. You can tell us all to leave if you really want. Just say the word."

Did she really want them to? She longed to be able to sleep in her own bed and not worry. She could handle money worries a whole lot better than the threat of George Carlisle. She wasn't going to allow money to get in the way of her security.

Sensing her hesitation, Kevin added, "Look, I know it's not perfect. What plan is? But at least once you're locked inside this house at night, you won't have to worry about what's outside trying to get in. I can check on you, make sure you get home okay and that you've got your doors locked. Then I can go home to my own bed for a good night's sleep. I'll be more alert in the morning to be able to do my job arresting your ex-husband. Once that happens, you won't have to worry at all anymore."

She thought about it a moment. "Knock yourself out, boys."

Mr. Stanasloski nodded. "It'll take a few hours with just the two of us working. But don't worry. When we're done, you won't even know we were here. You might want to find something to do for the day while we get the system installed. We'll do the alarm today. Ski will come by again tomorrow to finish putting in the camera system."

"Today may be a good day for you to finally get some work done on that boat of yours, Kevin," Ski called out as he left the room.

When Daria heard the sound of Ski and his father's boots on her wooden floors in the foyer, she said quietly, "You have a boat? You said you like to sail but you never mentioned a boat."

"Kevin's always complaining he never has enough time to get his sailboat finished. Never enough hours in the day."

"I can relate to that," Daria said. There were never enough hours for her to get what she wanted done on the house. But she hated the idea that her predicament was keeping Kevin from living his own life.

"Is that true?" she asked.

"I have an older sailboat in dry dock that I've been working on. It's seaworthy and has a lot of nice features. I'd like to do some serious sailing when the weather is better in the spring."

"Working on until you met me, you mean."

He shook his head. "Don't worry about it."

"You should be out doing something you enjoy, Kevin. Not babysitting me all the time."

"I won't lie. I love giving the boat my attention on the weekends. I enjoy being down at the marina. But there's plenty of time for that later."

Later was something that had no definite measure of time attached to it for Daria. Not while George and whomever else he might be connected to was still out there.

"You should go today," she said. "Ski and his dad are here. I'll be fine. There's no reason you should have to be stuck here with me. You should take a day to yourself and have some fun."

It may have been her imagination, but his expression faltered.

"You trying to get rid of me?"

"No. I just…feel bad you've been running yourself ragged these last few weeks."

"Regardless of what you may think, I don't feel stuck

when I'm with you. And after seeing you in this pretty dress, I thought maybe you'd decided to come to church with me today. You mentioned you might."

"Actually, that was the plan until the crew arrived. I just wasn't sure you'd still be going. You know, with all this going on."

The light that flashed in Kevin's eyes was immediate, as was his smile. "I am still planning to go. And I'd love it if you came with me."

"You sure you don't mind?"

"Not at all. In fact, if you want, we'll make a compromise. We'll go to church and you can meet some of the people there. I'll introduce you to the pastor over coffee and Danish. And then, if you want, we'll go down to the marina for the afternoon and do some work on the sailboat. That way we'll be out of Ski and his dad's way while they work. And I can get some boat time in. I can always use a hand."

"I suppose it's only fair," Daria said with a light chuckle. "You did help me with my house. Just let me grab a change of clothes."

The fresh air was doing her good, Daria realized. Unlike the night she found the bird on her door, Daria hadn't quite recovered from the break-in. It helped to get away from it for a few hours. She was looking forward to the distraction of meeting new people.

As she walked into church with Kevin, she caught more than a few glances from the women in the congregation. She and Kevin sat in a pew in the middle of the church and waited for the services to begin.

Daria felt only mildly out of place as she followed the service. Kevin opened a book and guided her through the prayers. She didn't know the words or the tune of the songs as everyone sang. But she followed along.

Her favorite part was the pastor's sermon. She listened to every word and thought about how it applied to her life. As she listened, a warm feeling enveloped her. As if she'd filled a space in her heart that had been empty.

When the service was over, everyone left the church and walked to the rectory where they were serving coffee and treats.

Kevin smiled and waved to people as they walked. It seemed as though he knew everyone.

"You hungry?" he asked her as they walked into the crowded room.

"A little," she said, smiling at a woman who'd been staring at her in church. She was pleased when the smile was returned with a quick nod, as if in approval.

"We need to move fast then," Kevin said, keeping his voice low. "Loretta Olsen has spotted you and it's only a matter of time before she makes her way to us to find out just who this beautiful woman is."

Daria giggled. "Who's Loretta Olsen?"

"She works in the church office. If Loretta had her way, she'd have your name, address and social security number to do a CORI check as soon as everyone left."

"Really?"

"Don't worry. She's a nice lady. Just likes to know who's attending church. Here she comes."

A short woman, who Daria decided was about the same age as her parents, came quickly through the crowd. "Kevin, there's plenty of pastries," the woman said when she reached them. "I know how much you like my apple spice cake."

"I'll stick to the coffee today, Loretta. Thanks just the same," he said.

"Aren't you going to introduce me to your friend? I'm Loretta Olsen. I work in the church office. I know every member of the church but don't believe I've seen you here before, Miss…"

"Call me Daria."

"Daria. An unusual name. Make sure you have some pastries. Jennifer Drake made that coffee roll."

Daria glanced at Kevin and smiled. "It all looks wonderful."

"Well, help yourself. Did you just move to town?" Loretta asked.

Having been warned by Kevin, Daria had the feeling she was about to be interrogated. But Loretta seemed nice enough.

Kevin took Daria by the hand, a gesture that didn't go unnoticed by Loretta. "I see Pastor Harrison. Let's go say hello." He turned to Loretta. "If you don't mind, Loretta. Good seeing you again."

"Oh, no. Go right ahead," she said.

As they walked toward the back of the room where the pastor was now conversing with some other church members, Kevin leaned closer to Daria and said, "Sorry about that. But Loretta is legendary for digging for information. Inside of an hour she would have known about every childhood friend you had from kindergarten all the way to your senior year of college, along with every town you lived in and the names of your professors."

Daria laughed. "That'd take all day and then some."

He introduced her to various people as they passed through the crowd. Everyone seemed so friendly and so willing to accept her that she didn't have a bit of apprehension.

Pastor Harrison, and the couple he was talking to, turned to Daria and Kevin as they approached. After quick introductions, Daria soon learned that Belinda and Jerry Tobin were both nurses at the local hospital.

"It's good to see you, Kevin," Jerry said, shaking Kevin's hand.

Despite not being a part of a church community before, Daria felt quite at home, making small talk and laughing with people she'd just met. No one questioned whether or not she belonged here. It was if they accepted her openly. She'd learned long ago how to make friends quickly. But there'd always been reserve held back on the other side. Today she felt none of that.

Belinda turned to Kevin and said, "We were just discussing the Christmas dinner, Kevin." Then turning to Daria, she added, "The church puts on a Christmas dinner early on Christmas Day for people in the community. Not just people who belong to our church. Everyone is welcome. There are a lot of people who don't feel like they have anywhere to go for Christmas, and the dinner is a way for them to be a part of the holidays even if they're missing out on being with family."

"Belinda has roped me into carving turkey for the last four years," Kevin said.

"Oh, you're always so good with the elderly women. They all love you."

Daria gave him a sidelong glance and smiled. She knew just how easy it had been for Kevin to win over Mrs. Hildebrand.

"We get a lot of elderly who can't travel far," Kevin said. "Jerry has even offered a van service to pick them up."

Jerry nodded. "It's what I'd want someone to do for my parents if they were alone."

"That's so sweet of you," Daria said.

Pastor Harrison slapped Jerry on the back. "It's a good community with a lot of wonderful people. Kevin told me the other day he might bring a friend with him to church this week. I'm glad you decided to come with him."

Daria glanced in Kevin's direction and he knew he was in trouble. But he couldn't say that he was sorry he'd talked to Pastor Harrison. He'd known the pastor since he was a kid. Pastor Harrison had been a huge comfort when Lucy was killed. His guidance was important to Kevin.

He'd prayed for guidance with the pastor and that guidance had led Daria here with him today. He was glad he had.

Daria's sweet laugh and sunshine smile had dug under his skin, settling into places in his soul he didn't even know existed until now. Having her here with him today opened up a place in his heart he'd forced shut.

He thought Daria might be angry. But she surprised him when she said, "I'm really glad he invited me to come. I loved your sermon."

"You're one of the rare people who actually listened to everything I said. I noticed you immediately."

Daria smiled.

"Will you be spending the holidays with your family?" Belinda asked Daria.

She gave a quick glance to Kevin, then to Belinda. "No, my parents are in Mexico."

Pastor Harrison's expression turned serious. "Surely you won't be spending Christmas alone."

Before Daria could answer, Kevin stepped in. "I

thought I might convince Daria to spend the holiday with me."

Belinda's eyes widened. "Oh, this is perfect! Why don't you come down with Kevin for the Christmas dinner here. We can always use an extra hand."

Kevin's first instinct was to decline for Daria. There'd be a lot of people at the Christmas dinner. This was Daria's first visit to the church and the last thing he wanted was to overwhelm her, causing her to run in the opposite direction. But then she surprised him.

"I'd love to come."

"Are you sure?" Kevin asked.

"Why not? I'd like to help out. I was going to be alone anyway. This way we can have a little fun, have Christmas turkey here and spend the rest of the afternoon working on the house. That is, if you still want to spend the day with me."

"Great!" Belinda said, clapping her hands together.

Kevin took a moment to talk with Pastor Harrison when Daria excused herself to go change clothes in the restroom.

"It's okay to take your guard down," Pastor Harrison said. "She seems like a sweet girl."

"Not with an ex-husband who is determined to kill her," Kevin said in a low voice that others couldn't hear.

"I'll pray for you both."

"I appreciate that." Even the comfort of the pastor's words didn't shake the feeling that perhaps they were all underestimating just how dangerous George Carlisle was. Determined not to let it ruin the rest of the day, Kevin offered those fears up to the Lord and waited for Daria.

As they walked across the marina parking lot to where Kevin's sailboat was in dry dock, Kevin decided that insisting Daria come with him to the marina for the day was the right idea.

A gust of wind pushed the door against the building as he tried to open it. "Let me hold the door for you," he said. "With this December wind, it's liable to fly back at you just as you're walking through."

"The water's pretty choppy today. I'm surprised there are boats out at all," Daria said, looking out into Narragansett Bay.

Once inside with the door securely shut tight, the wind coming off the bay whistled through the rafters.

"Some people are braver than me," Kevin said with a chuckle. "Either that or they have a cast-iron stomach."

With her scarf pulled tight around her neck, Daria looked around. "I've never been out on the water before."

"Yeah? Maybe we can remedy that in the spring."

Daria walked into the bay and looked around at the covered boats until her eyes settled on his.

"Let me guess. Your boat is *Her Gypsy Heart?*" she said, pointing to the thirty-two-foot sailboat sitting up on the trailer at the end of the bay.

"That's the one," he said, beaming with pride. "I still have a few little odds and ends to finish up the inside cabin. It's a lot easier to do it over the winter in dry dock than trying to steady a drill out on the water."

"I can imagine."

He glanced at her then, saw the vacant look she'd had earlier had been replaced by anticipation and intrigue.

"You've been fixing your boat up by yourself?"

"Trying to. I bought it almost four years ago. Tyler—he's the guy you met earlier in the office—used to be a cop."

"And now he manages the marina?"

"Yeah, but when I met him he was Jake's partner. Anyway, he'd just started working here when this old girl came sailing in. She was barely seaworthy then."

Daria waited as Kevin dragged a ladder to the side of the boat and climbed it, then proceeded to undo the boat cover and peel it back so the deck was exposed. He turned to extend a hand to help her board, but instead of coming toward him, she put a hand on her hip and took the length of the boat in with a long, slow perusal.

With a crooked smile, she said, "She doesn't look very old to me."

"Old girl or not, she's my pride and joy. She's a beauty now, but you should have seen her the day I bought her. Jake thought I was nuts. One of these days I'm going to sail her down the coast to the Florida Keys. See how she does."

Daria was looking at him in a way that told him she understood. And for the first time since he met her, he understood something important about her, too. Daria's connection to her house was similar to what he felt for this boat.

But unlike Daria, Kevin knew his sailboat was just an object. The joy it gave him was something he felt deep inside, but it couldn't complete him the way Daria seemed to believe her house could complete her.

She curled her fingers around the rungs of the ladder. "You've got some Gypsy blood, Kevin."

"Nomadic, maybe. I really don't know if I'll ever do it. My dad and I talk about taking a scuba lesson and sailing for buried treasure in the Caribbean. It drives my mother crazy."

"She doesn't like the idea?"

Extending his hand, he helped Daria climb onto the

deck. "Not unless there is a bottle of Dramamine handy. Who knows? It still remains to be seen if *Her Gypsy Heart* can even handle a voyage that long. When I'm working on her though, or when I'm out on the water, staring out into that vast ocean beyond the bay, I have these fantasies of sailing her around the world."

"Really? You'd give up everything you have here just to sail around the world alone?"

"Well, maybe not alone. But it's not like there is a whole lot keeping me here anymore. My parents have moved down south. My sister is married to a navy man and hasn't been back to Rhode Island for any length of time in years. I mostly go visit her and the kids wherever Larry's stationed. It's just me and my little boat here now."

She was quiet a minute and he wondered what had brought that on.

"Come on. I'll show you around."

TWELVE

Daria stepped down into the cabin of *Her Gypsy Heart* and looked around in awe. When Kevin had helped her work on the house, she hadn't realized he was a craftsman. Sure, it was clear after a few minutes he was good with her tools. But what he'd done restoring the sailboat was exquisite.

It was true she'd never set foot on a boat before today, but she'd seen plenty of pictures and she knew good work when she saw it. As she walked around, she admired all the little things Kevin had done to make it his. Having worked these last months renovating her own house, she could appreciate the little details a true craftsman would take pride in. And there was much to be proud of where *Her Gypsy Heart* was concerned.

Still, once they got down to work, Daria was most intrigued by how Kevin behaved. He seemed much calmer here on the boat than when he was sitting outside on the curb by her house. This was truly his sanctuary. She felt honored that he'd shared it with her.

They took a quick break, having a root beer while sitting on deck. They'd been quietly working the last hour and she'd spent the time concentrating on the

features of Kevin's face, something she always believed
told its own story. Every line had a story.

"How did you get that scar over your eyebrow?" she
finally asked when he caught her staring. She'd noticed
it the other night while he slept. Now her curiosity got
the better of her.

Kevin lifted his eyes as if he could actually see the
scar, then chuckled deeply. "You don't want to know."

"Oh, no, you don't. Now you have to tell me."

He finished the rest of his drink and set the empty
bottle on the seat next to him.

"It's no big deal."

"Then you should have no problem telling me the
story."

"I was trying to climb the trellis on the side of my
parents' house and, uh, didn't make it."

"Oh, no. How far did you fall?"

"Far enough. I needed eight stitches."

Daria put her hand to her head in sympathy. "Ouch."

"You don't know the half of it." He leaned forward,
resting his elbows on his knees. "I remember the
emergency-room doctor wanting to shave my eyebrow
to get a nice clean stitch and my mother arguing with
him that she didn't want me to end up like those movie
actresses who shaved their eyebrows and then didn't
have them grow back." He laughed, loud and rich,
making his voice echo in the confines of the marina. "All
she could imagine was me walking around with one
eyebrow for the rest of my life."

Daria couldn't help but laugh, too.

"So she took her tweezers out of her purse and started
plucking the hair around my wound. Dad got all hot

under the collar and started screaming about how he drew the line at lipstick and eye shadow."

"All for climbing the trellis. What were you doing up there, saving a kitten or something?"

His expression faltered just a fraction. "No, I wanted to check on my sister."

Daria eyed him suspiciously. "Spying on your sister got you eight stitches? I hope it was worth it."

He shrugged, but Daria could tell they'd just touched some troubled waters.

She allowed the silence to linger and not push Kevin in a direction that was uncomfortable. If he wanted to talk about it he could. This was a safe harbor. There had to be someplace on this earth that was safe. When it seemed the time had well passed on the subject, Kevin looked at her, his eyes serious and intense.

"In a way, you remind me of Lucy," he said quietly.

There was just a hint of a smile on his face that let her know that Lucy, whoever she was, had been special to Kevin.

"I thought your sister's name was Judy."

"Lucy was her best friend. She lived next door."

"Ah, the picture is starting to come into view now. So you had it bad for your big sister's best friend and you climbed the trellis to spy on both of them?"

But Kevin didn't laugh or even crack a smile. He just looked at her the way he had that first morning when he'd asked her to pack her things and move far away where George couldn't find her.

"It was the day Lucy was killed by her ex-boyfriend."

Daria gasped.

"Judy had locked herself in her bedroom and Mom was afraid she was going to do something drastic.

They'd been such good friends. I figured I could handle climbing up the trellis and getting into the window. I mean, Judy and I fought, but she wasn't going to push me away. Not at that height, anyway. Knowing Judy, she'd have been really ticked off and yelled at me, but at least I'd have made it into the room. I figured I'd talk to her, help her through what she was feeling. I mean, we were all going through it, too."

He smirked then and shrugged. "I did have it bad for Lucy. She was kinda cool. She didn't push me away like I was some geeky kid, which I was at that time. All feet and arms."

Daria couldn't imagine it. But there had to have been a time before Kevin had grown into himself, gone from boy to man.

"Anyway, I only made it about halfway up the trellis before it started to break away from the house. I lost my grip and fell into a shrub."

"That probably got your sister out of her room," Daria said quietly.

"And how. It wasn't the way I'd planned, but she ended up flying out of the house and running to the front lawn. As soon as she realized I didn't break my neck, she stood there and yelled at me for scaring her. I felt like a real idiot and then I just felt bad for her. I mean, she'd just lost her best friend."

"What happened?"

Kevin looked at her directly. "Do you really want to know?"

Daria wasn't sure if she did. But she'd come this far and she wasn't about to stop him.

"Lucy had broken up with her boyfriend of three years. All through their relationship, Jimmy had been what she'd called a 'gentle soul.' It started like it always does. Innocent. You've never seen him angry and then something inside him snaps. I remember Jimmy standing out in the rain one night, just staring at her window and crying like a baby."

Daria could easily picture it in her mind. "He loved her."

Kevin groaned. "He murdered her, Daria. That isn't love."

"I know. But he just came after her? Just like that? No warning?"

"A lot of times, there is no warning at all. But looking back, there were warning signs. Judy told me Jimmy used to get angry and grab Lucy, leaving bruises on her. Lucy would always say she fell or was just a klutz. Everyone believed her. It got worse toward the end of their relationship, which is why Lucy broke it off with him. But I never saw any of that. Jimmy always seemed like a good guy."

Daria leaned closer to him. She wasn't sure if she was trying to comfort him or herself. But she felt warmed by the closeness, by how she always felt safe with Kevin.

"One night, about a month after they'd broken up, Jimmy stood out in the rain and kept yelling for Lucy. Just calling her name until her parents called the police. I remember thinking the guy looked so pathetic. Judy was on the phone with Lucy because Lucy was scared right up until the police came. Part of me had some stupid kid fantasy that if Jimmy was out of the picture it would open the door for me. Lucy was really nice. Not just pretty, but a nice girl who actually took the time to sit with me and talk to me like I was something more than her best friend's geeky younger brother."

"That's not stupid. You were a kid and Lucy was your first crush. No one ever forgets their first real crush.

"What happened to Lucy? Did her boyfriend came back after the police left?"

"No. Jimmy waited about a month after that night before he drove to our high school to see Lucy again. Judy didn't want me walking home with her friends because she didn't want her cool friends to see me with her." He shrugged. "I have to admit, me and my friends had played some pretty wild tricks on Judy, so I deserved it.

"Anyway, the two girls were walking ahead of us. My buddy and I figured we were in a good position to eavesdrop on whatever conversation they were having. Keeping a respectable distance to pretend we weren't tailing them, of course."

"Of course."

"And then Jimmy pulled up along the curb. I remember the smile on his face. He seemed harmless, not at all pathetic like he'd been that night on the lawn. But looking back I always wondered if he was smiling because he knew right then he was going to kill Lucy."

Kevin sighed, thinking of how things could have turned out if he'd only done something that day. Lucy probably would have gone on to grow into a stunning woman, married, had a family of her own, just like Judy had. All that was snuffed out that afternoon.

Daria was watching him intently. It was important to him that she know how determined Lucy's situation made him to ensure that Daria's problem with her ex-husband didn't turn into a repeat of Lucy's death. He'd seen the same thing play out many times over the years. Maybe it didn't always end in a murder. But he'd gone on countless calls where a woman was beaten by a so-called loved one and refused to leave.

"Jimmy said he just wanted to talk, to let her know he was okay with everything. He was going to drive her to work at the market. Judy said goodbye and kept walking."

He looked down at the bottle next to him, which was spilling the dregs of root beer onto the bench. He grabbed a paper towel and quickly wiped it away.

"They found Lucy later that night in the Dumpster behind the market. She'd never even made it in to work."

Daria covered her face with her hands. "That is truly horrible. For all of you."

It *had* been horrible. Over fifteen years later he still remembered what it felt like to hear that Lucy was dead.

"Knowing how important your faith is to you, I imagine it was a big help to get you through that difficult time."

"Yes, it was. I've learned not to ask the Lord why, because some things are just too senseless to understand. But for us, life went on eventually. For Lucy, it didn't. After that night when Jimmy wouldn't leave her house, the police and her parents urged Lucy to get a restraining order, but she thought everyone was overreacting. Even though he'd hurt her before, she trusted Jimmy. Until he killed her."

Daria sat up straight. "That's why you want me to leave so badly."

He nodded. "And your situation is a thousand times worse because George has given us a warning sign as big and bold as a highway billboard. We know without a doubt that he's a threat. We just don't know when or where he'll strike."

Daria shook her head as if she was trying to dislodge the image from her brain. "No one other than Judy knew Lucy was being hurt by this guy?"

"No. He'd sat politely at Lucy's dinner table next to

Lucy hundreds of times. Jimmy had been to my house just as many times and I never would have believed the guy was capable of hurting anyone. But Lucy had confided in Judy and I think that was one more reason Judy took Lucy's death so hard. She always wished she would have told someone instead of keeping Lucy's secret until it was too late."

Daria went to stand, but fell back to the seat as if she was unsteady on her feet. It was clear the story had rocked her. "The alarm system—"

"It's only a means of alerting us if George or someone else tries to break into the house again whether you're home or not. I don't want your ex near you, Daria. I won't give him the chance to hurt you."

"I'm not Lucy," she said directly.

Kevin drew in a deep breath. "I know that. But George has made his intentions clear, and he's a dangerous man. And while we haven't been able to prove his association with anyone worse than a loan shark, I'm pretty sure he knows some dangerous people—dangerous enough to find a real hit man this time. We need to get him put away before that can happen."

"Gambling."

"What?"

He was still processing the omission when she suddenly stood up.

"When you asked me that first day if I knew anything about why George needed the money from the loan shark, I was telling you the truth. But I've always suspected George had a gambling problem. I never knew why George had a lot of money sometimes, and sometimes would be so heavily in debt. He never talked to me about it."

She turned to Kevin.

"What is it?" he asked.

"You said you wanted to pull an Al Capone on George. I don't know enough about his dealings to give you any real information. We filed separate tax returns. His idea. Looking back, I realize I would have known more if we'd filed together."

"You never saw his tax returns?"

She shook her head and sighed.

"Unlike me, George liked to live a large lifestyle. I always knew he liked nice things, but it got worse after he finished college and got a job.

"When we got divorced and submitted our financial records, George didn't have two nickels to rub together. At least on paper. So where did all that money he was always spending come from?"

"Maybe he just spent it all. You said he liked to live beyond his means."

"Yeah, but according to his court statements, he didn't earn enough for the kind of money he was throwing around. The numbers didn't add up. So where was he getting it?"

Kevin thought about it a moment. "If he has gambling winnings he didn't report to the IRS, that's an angle, but not one that will necessarily land him in jail. I could have Jake check into it. See if he frequents any of the casinos in the neighboring states. But if he's into private games, I'm not sure he'll come up on any surveillance tapes. Most people who high roll want anonymity."

The tension had returned and although Kevin had enjoyed relaxing with Daria, he didn't want to forget that George was still out there, possibly plotting another hit with someone else.

Lord, Daria looks so small and fragile right now. If it is Your will, help me find the path that will lead to bringing her safety and peace of mind again.

"I love the way you do that," she said, breaking into his thoughts.

"What?"

"You were praying, weren't you?"

It amazed him that Daria could read him so well. "Yes."

"You were like that in church today."

"What about you? You said you've never really been inside church before, but you seemed right at home there. I kept wondering what you were thinking."

"I don't know how to describe it." A blush colored her cheeks.

"You don't have to be embarrassed."

"I'm not, it's just hard to explain. I listened to the pastor and listened to the prayers. I didn't know any, but I listened and I had this overwhelming feeling that I...wasn't alone. Not so much because of all the people in the room. It was different. I can't really describe it. I know it probably sounds crazy."

"No, it sounds nice."

She smiled. "I'd like to go back there. I wasn't looking forward to Christmas because I thought I'd be alone. But now I'm really looking forward to going back to the church."

"You don't have to be in church to feel God's presence."

She nodded. "I think I'm beginning to see that."

His heart swelled. Today Daria had taken a huge step in her faith journey. And with it, he felt some hope that she was on her way to accepting the Lord into her life.

And then her face changed. The quiet calm that seemed to have come over her for that brief moment when they were talking about how she felt in church was replaced by fear again.

Kevin had the overwhelming urge to hold Daria in his arms. He wanted to keep her safe so nothing could touch her, nothing could hurt her. Today had brought him incredible hope that he and Daria could move forward with their feelings now that she was starting to accept Christ in her life. But with that hope also came alarming fear that she could be snatched away from him like Lucy.

The alarm system Ski and his dad were installing today was only a safety net. It wasn't a guarantee.

Unable to watch her fear any longer, Kevin stood and drew Daria into his arms. She seemed to fit so perfectly there. As she lifted her face to him, he gently placed his lips against hers. Responding, she wrapped her arms around his shoulders and returned the kiss. It felt so right. When they parted, he looked down into Daria's eyes and thought of nothing but contentment, happiness. How could any man ever think of harming an amazing woman like Daria?

Daria must have felt him tense and she sighed in response. Resting her head on his shoulder, she said, "He's never going to stop, is he?"

"I don't know."

He looked into Daria's amazing eyes, seeing the deeper meaning in the way she looked at him. He'd do just about anything to stand there and look at her beautiful face all night. Her smile had penetrated his every thought, every second of the day since the moment they'd met.

An ominous mood settled over Kevin, breaking the peacefulness of the day. His instincts told him definitively that George would strike again. He only prayed that he'd make it to Daria in time to stop George or his hired gun from succeeding.

THIRTEEN

Ski and his dad were gone by the time they'd made their way back to Daria's house. It was just as well, Daria thought as Kevin pulled his SUV into the driveway behind her truck. She wasn't used to people parading through her house. And after the day she'd shared with Kevin, she didn't want to make small talk.

It was snowing again. As they walked from the truck to the front door, snowflakes stuck to her coat and her hair. The front-porch light was on, but the inside lights were dark.

"I asked Ski to replace the front-door lock if he had time. Seems like he did, because the lock looks brand-new." Kevin handed Daria a key and a slip of paper. "This is your alarm key code. Punch it in as soon as you walk through the door and it will deactivate the alarm. Remember, you only have twenty seconds to disarm it. Put on all the motion sensors for the doors and windows as soon as you're set inside. Shut off the sensors for the rooms while you're awake. You can put them back on when you go to sleep. Just don't sleepwalk or you'll wake up the whole neighborhood."

She chuckled, but felt a sense of anxiousness. It wasn't

about the house or her safety. It was about Kevin. She'd had a hard time thinking of anything but Kevin all day.

"I guess now that I have this new handy dandy alarm system, there really isn't a need for you to continue watching over me as much. Is there?"

Kevin cleared his throat. "You don't get rid of me that easy, Daria. But you're right, there is no need for me to be sitting at the curb tonight. I will be here first thing tomorrow morning though."

"No one but you and Ski have this code?"

"Just us. But if the alarm goes off, you'll have your own army of cops on your doorstep within minutes."

"What about you?" she said softly. "Will you come running too? I kind of liked having you close by."

"I'll be the first one here."

Daria unlocked the front door, surprised she didn't have to struggle with the lock. Once inside the foyer, she quickly punched in the alarm code, checking the slip of paper to make sure she'd entered it correctly. Kevin walked into the house behind her and turned the lights on, illuminating the hallway.

"Go ahead and set the doors and windows to get a feel for the system until you're comfortable with it. I'm going to take a quick look around."

She practiced setting and disarming the alarm several times, taking note of which lights on the panel turned on and shut off when she pushed the buttons. When Kevin came back to the foyer, she turned on the alarm for the doors and windows.

"I hope you don't mind. I called for a pizza. That way neither one of us has to cook," Kevin said.

"I appreciate that. I'm starved."

"You look tired, too," he said, pulling her into a warm

embrace. Daria relished the feeling. The day had been perfect and the thought that it would end too quickly was disappointing. She was glad he'd taken the initiative to call for takeout. Although it had been a major annoyance at first, she liked having Kevin here. She'd been alone in her house for so long, but even after these few short weeks, the house felt empty without him.

Kevin followed her into the living room. "I found another box of ornaments upstairs and I want to finish decorating this tree," she said.

With a flip of a switch the Christmas-tree lights went on. Red, green, gold and white lights started to flicker.

She turned to find Kevin watching her. In his eyes, she saw the same deep emotion she'd seen down at the marina when he'd kissed her.

Daria handed him a box of ornaments and pulled a few hooks from a small package to attach to them.

"Are you really serious about wanting to just take off and sail around the world?" she asked.

"Yeah. When you're out on the ocean and it's just you, the water and the sky, it's amazing. It feels like the world and its problems can't touch you."

"Or find you," she said. "George wouldn't find me."

"That would be a bonus. I'd love to have you all to myself." He reached up and kissed her lips, warm and soft. "Come on. You don't think sailing around the world together would be fun?"

She looked at him with serious blue eyes. "I'm not a gypsy anymore, Kevin. I left that kind of living behind when I grew up. I love the idea of going sailing with you someday. I love being with you. But I want to come home, too. To this home."

She'd been thinking a lot about that conversation at

the marina and their time at church this morning. "I'm surprised you'd want to leave all this behind. I mean, it's clear you know just about everyone in your church and they all know you. I've never experienced anything like that. You were right. When I was there with you this morning I felt so much a part of everything, like they all just accepted me in with no question."

Kevin placed an ornament high on the tree and waited for her to hand him another. She slipped a hook on an ornament from the box and handed it to him.

"Everyone who wants to accept the Lord into their life is welcome there. I guess it's just a given to them that you felt that way."

When a short silence hung in the air a little too long not to notice, she said, "You always stop short of asking me. Why is that?"

"Asking what?"

"If I believe in God. You tell me how you feel about your faith. You asked me about how I felt in church today. But you stop short of asking me if my feelings have changed. If I believe. You said that was important to you."

Kevin thought a moment. "It's very important to me. But faith is a personal thing between you and the Lord. It's not something anyone else can make happen for you. My faith has seen me and my family through some rough times over the years. Without being able to pray and know that God was listening, feeling His grace, I don't know where I'd be."

She thought about it for a moment herself. She had felt something special earlier today when she'd been at the church with Kevin. She didn't know what it was and couldn't define it. But it was there and it felt good.

A soft sigh escaped Daria's lips. "You're lucky."

"Why?"

"You were raised with all of that. I don't even know how to pray."

He seemed to sense her embarrassment, but didn't show any sign of judgment toward her. "There are a lot of formal prayers. But it doesn't have to be that way. Prayer is just a conversation between you and the Lord. That's all. There's no right or wrong. You just have to have an open heart."

Her heart had opened up today. Was that what it was like to accept the Lord into your life? She didn't know. But she wanted to know more.

"Your faith grounds you. You've dug in roots here and yet you have no problem just picking up and leaving. My parents were like that. I'd come home one day from school feeling happy and there'd be boxes all packed in the kitchen ready to be loaded into the car. I always hated leaving and moving somewhere else. I'd love to have what you have here in Providence. But I guess so much of what you have here is dug so deeply inside you that it doesn't matter where you are. You'll always feel home."

"I suppose you're right."

"Like I said, you're lucky. I never had that."

"You could. But it has to be up to you."

The air flowing between them seemed to crackle. Kevin's arm snaked out and curled around her neck, drawing her closer to him until she was pressed against his chest. With a ragged intake of breath, his mouth came down over hers. In his arms she trembled with the new feelings he evoked. She felt safe in Kevin's arms. And for the first time, her heart swelled and she knew without a doubt, she was falling in love.

The doorbell rang and Kevin groaned. "I'm starving, but that was bad timing. I don't suppose we could get the delivery guy to drive around the block so I can kiss you a little more."

A giggle bubbled up Daria's throat as Kevin kissed her again.

"I'll get the door," he said.

"Wait, take the code. I put the alarm on."

"Good thinking. I didn't order enough pizza for the entire police force if the alarm goes off."

With the Christmas lights twinkling around her, she watched as Kevin went to the door. Her heart felt so light and so full. She was falling in love with Kevin and he was opening her heart to a new way of life. How could she possibly fear George when she had Kevin in her life?

The daisies she'd picked up at the corner florist were an extravagance Daria hadn't allowed herself in a long time. The prime rib she'd paid way too much for was definitely way over the top, but she didn't care. She'd been thinking all day about how a candlelight dinner with Kevin would be a nice start to the week.

He'd left her last night with a lot of questions still on his mind. It had become crystal clear to her as she lay in bed thinking of what her life would be like if Kevin was a permanent part of it.

Kevin was a man of incredible integrity and unwavering faith in God. It seemed only likely that he would be with a woman who shared that faith. Daria wanted to be that woman. And tonight at dinner she would tell him that for sure.

A deeper, startling revelation she came to was that she wanted to know the Lord even if Kevin wasn't in her life. She'd found something she hadn't realized was missing. Kevin had brought her to the Lord and now she didn't want to turn back.

Daria had managed to run all her errands during lunch so she would have extra time to prepare dinner before Kevin arrived. Marla had been too preoccupied talking about a new guy she'd met at the gym for her to notice the goofy grin Daria knew she'd been wearing all day. Daria had to admit she was relieved. She no longer had to worry about Marla hooking up with George and possibly getting hurt.

Ski would be at the house waiting for her today to install the camera system. That meant that Kevin was coming over to her house to be with her, not to protect her. Things had changed between them. She had changed, too. After spending the day with Kevin, going to church with him, meeting the people he'd known his whole life, she'd felt something click.

She wasn't foolish enough to think she could have the kind of relationship with the Lord that Kevin had, or any of the other people she'd met yesterday. He'd had years to come to the place that he was in his faith. But as he said, it takes a first step to let God in, and she'd taken that first step yesterday.

She found herself looking forward to Christmas and to helping out at the community center. Being with Kevin. If she had to deal with an alarm system in her house to be able to finally stay in the home she'd dreamed of for years, to have the sense of roots and community that Kevin had, then she'd put up with it. And hopefully, with Kevin's help and the Lord's guidance, they'd find a way to stop this threat George had over her.

Ski was waiting in the driveway when she got home, already geared up with his tool belt and wire. Daria waved to him as she got out of the car and grabbed her bags.

"Sorry I needed an extra day for this. I know you're eager to have your house all to yourself," Ski said.

"I don't mind." Hoisting the bag up in her arms, she made her way to the front door and unlocked it. She dropped the bag to the floor and quickly disarmed the alarm.

"I already have the camera mounted on the front," Ski said. "I need to mount the other camera out back and then connect them."

"You've been working with your dad on alarms for a while, huh?"

"Since I was old enough to hold a drill."

"How long have you been a police officer?"

Ski shrugged. "I'm a babe in the woods compared to some of the other officers. Jake and Kevin have been great about teaching me. If I know Kevin, he probably didn't tell you about my mistake the night of the sting with your ex."

"What mistake?"

"I moved in too fast and tried to arrest George Carlisle before Kevin gave me the signal. It was my fault the charges were dropped. I know Kevin would have done it different and your ex would probably be in jail by now."

She smiled. Ski was a nice young man. And she couldn't thank him enough for what he'd done to help her over the last few weeks.

"I don't think Kevin would trust you with the job you're doing if he didn't have complete faith in your ability. Don't be too hard on yourself."

Ski smiled. In actuality, he was probably only about five or six years younger than she was.

He thumbed toward the back of the house. "If you hear any noise, it's just me out back."

Daria had just enough time to prepare the roast and vegetables and get them started in the oven. A few times she was startled by the sound of a drill against the clapboard or a bang downstairs but she stayed out of the way, hoping Ski finished up before Kevin got there.

After collecting her glass vase, Daria reached across the counter to grab the daisies she'd picked up during lunch. She whistled in the kitchen.

Before she could fill the vase with water, she heard the front door open and then close. It couldn't be Ski because he'd been working down in the basement with the electrical panel.

"You're early," she said, spinning around expecting to see Kevin.

"I remember a time when that smile greeted me every day. I kind of miss seeing it."

Daria's heart plunged in fear at seeing George again. Panic coursed through her. She'd never felt fear like this when she'd been married to George and she didn't like the feeling now. Where was Ski?

"You shouldn't be here, George," she said, glancing past him.

"He's not there."

"Who?"

"That young cop who's been following me. Your plumber's wrench went to good use."

Her breath hitched in her throat. "What...what did you do to Ski?"

"Why the sudden frown? Were you expecting someone else?"

"That's none of your business."

"We're married, Daria. Anything that makes you unhappy is my business."

Irritation curled through her. "We're divorced."

"Yes, we are. But I don't think I got my fair share of what's coming to me in the divorce."

Daria glanced passed George again, listening for Kevin's SUV. But she heard nothing.

George sneered. "I know you're expecting him, Daria. Are you going to have that cop move in with you now? It wasn't enough for him to park himself on your street corner. He has to move into your house now, too?"

She felt her hands tremble as she gripped the counter. How could George have known Kevin had been spending his nights in the car in front of her house? He couldn't know this unless he'd been watching.

"Stop it, George."

"You know, you hurt my feelings, Daria," he said, his voice dripping with sarcasm. "You didn't keep those beautiful flowers I gave you. You always loved those flowers."

"Get out of my house, George."

"You and I both know you can lock me out, but I'm going to get in. Your little friend out there might be good with a drill and a wrench." George's face twisted into a sneer. "Well, maybe not *that* good with a wrench. But even though you didn't keep my pretty little flowers, I still heard every word you said about me."

Confusion swirled in her mind as she tried to understand him. George was insane. And then it hit her. "You bugged my house?"

"Don't worry. I managed to get the information I needed. And you thought I'd hurt poor Marla. Tsk, tsk. She was a bore like always, but a highly useful vehicle for getting what I needed to get done."

Kevin and Daria had spoken about Marla outside. How could George have heard what they'd said?

She glanced at her purse on the kitchen table and bolted to grab it, but George got there first. "You're cold," he teased. Picking up her coat, which she'd draped over the back of the kitchen chair, he added, "I'm getting warmer. You left this in your office the day I asked Marla to lunch. You may want to check the lining, because there's a tiny, tiny tear in it."

"Where you planted a listening device." Pressing herself back against the counter, she looked around and wondered how many other microphones had been planted in her house.

"How else would I have known what you were doing? Knowing when the alarm would be off made it easier for me to plan when to come visit you. This fix-it cop you have here now is less formidable than your friend Officer Gordon."

George reached down and started wrenching through what was left in the grocery bag she'd left on the table.

"What is this? Candles? Looks like you're planning a nice romantic dinner and you forgot to invite me."

"George, if you don't leave now…"

His face was dark. "What? You'll call your cop friend? I don't think so. You've had your way for too long. Now it's my turn to call the shots. Or at least, the *hits*."

Daria flinched. *Lord, please let George be lying about hurting Ski. I don't want him to be hurt because of me.*

"Don't worry about the cop." George sneered. "Unlike you, he'll be fine. But now it's your turn to pay."

FOURTEEN

It was almost dark when Kevin made it to Daria's house. He tried not to read anything into why Ski's car was parked in the driveway with the front door still slightly ajar, leaving the inside light on.

He parked his SUV on the curb as he had many times before and looked around. Maybe Ski's arms were full and he'd forgotten to close the door. But Ski wasn't usually this careless.

He climbed out of the car and walked up the driveway toward the brick pathway.

The screen door opened and shut with a gust of wind. A wave of uneasiness hit Kevin square in the chest. Something was stuck there, keeping the door ajar. Ski wouldn't keep the front door open like that.

The hairs on the back of his neck stood to life and dread tumbled down upon him. He stared into the night and listened.

There was no noise. Spot wasn't barking. Not even when he'd gotten out of the SUV. The dog had always howled, loud enough to be heard from within the confines of the house. Now there was silence.

Kevin advanced toward Ski's car and found him

lying in the front seat, his foot dangling outside just enough to keep the door ajar. His hand was stretched out as if he'd been reaching for the handset on his police radio. With the light from the dashboard, Kevin saw the blood that was draining from Ski's head. He'd been struck with some type of large object.

Yanking the door open, Kevin quickly checked for a pulse and was relieved to find one. Ski was alive. *Thank You, Lord, he's alive.* Now where was Daria?

With no time to lose, Kevin quickly grabbed the police radio and his gun from his holster at the same time.

"This is Detective Gordon. Officer down. I need backup at 72 Hitchcock Street along with an ambulance."

Every bit of his training told him to wait for backup. It was never a good idea for an officer to enter a building alone where a violent crime had been committed. But nothing, no amount of police training, was going to keep him from going inside to find Daria.

With his gun drawn in front of him, he stepped up the front porch. Blood hammered in his ears as he bounded through the front door and into the hallway. The scent of blood drifted to his nose. Despite the cold, a bead of sweat sprang to his face.

As he moved slowly down the hall, the roar of his blood pounding through his veins made him dizzy. The stickiness he felt on the floor looked like drops of blood. Kevin knew immediately he'd just compromised a crime scene. But he had to know if Daria was in there and if it was her blood or Ski's.

Gripping his gun tighter in the palm of his hand, he inched his way down the hall, listening for movement. When he reached the kitchen, he lightly ran his hand up

the wall and flicked on the light switch. The sudden
glare stung his eyes and made him blink.

What he found in the kitchen made his body turn
cold. There was blood everywhere, smeared on the
newly painted hallway walls and on the old linoleum
kitchen floor.

He glanced back down the hall he'd just walked and
almost dropped to his knees, shuddering. A dark stretch
of smeared blood streaked the wall along with handprints.
His bloodstained footprints trailed along another set of
prints down the hallway and led to the kitchen. With his
eyes, he followed the path leading to his shoes. Another
large set of footprints and a smaller set that looked like
the size of a woman's running along the same path he'd
just taken in what looked like a chaotic pattern and…

Breathing hard, he screamed, "Daria!"

In the middle of the floor in a huge heap was a white
tablecloth soaking up the blood. White flower pedals
were pulled apart and scattered all over the floor among
broken glass.

Kevin closed his eyes as a quick prayer escaped his
lips. His throat constricted. *Daria. Not my sweet Daria.*

Minutes later, Kevin stood outside Daria's house as
crime-scene investigators crawled all over the yard and
the interior looking for evidence. One of them walked
over to Kevin.

"Detective Gordon. We found your bloody footprints
all over the hallway and kitchen. I hope you're not too
attached to your shoes."

He shook his head, glanced down at his feet. He'd
taken off his shoes almost immediately when he realized
Daria wasn't in the house. He knew they were going to

need to match the shoe print against the second set in the kitchen. "I left them in the kitchen. You can take them."

Office Johnson came up behind him with Captain Jorgensen. "We talked to a few of the neighbors. They all know Detective Gordon's SUV. Mrs. Parsons said she noticed another car here earlier, but I think she's talking about Ski's. She also heard some arguing and then heard the car speed away."

"Did she call it in?" Kevin asked.

"No, said she was trying to mind her own business."

Kevin's every attempt to keep himself emotionally detached was a losing battle. "I can't say I blame her," he finally said. "This neighborhood is used to seeing and hearing a lot of things. When it happens too often, it becomes routine."

"She does remember seeing Daria come home and then hearing a car speed down the street. Said she remembered it because she was angry someone would drive that fast down this side street, especially a neighbor."

Kevin closed his eyes and sighed. "What about Mrs. Hildebrand, the neighbor next door?"

"She said she heard the same argument as Mrs. Parsons but was too worried about her dog." Matt propped his hands on his hips. "And right now she's quite upset. Seems her dog was poisoned in what looks like an attempt to shut him up during the attack."

"The dog was poisoned?"

"Yeah, but he should be okay. He was given just enough to keep him out of the way and keep the neighbor preoccupied."

"Whoever did this knew Spot was there."

"Most likely. One of our officers is bringing Mrs. Hildebrand to the vet to have the dog checked out and write up a report." Matt pulled Kevin aside, out of earshot of the other officers. "Look, I know how personal this has gotten for you, but you need to stay focused. Walking through that house without backup was—"

"Stupid," he said, shaking his head. "Yeah, I know. But isn't that what you did?"

"Yeah," Matt said quietly. "And look what it got me."

The paramedics loaded Ski onto a stretcher and into the ambulance. The gash on his head was bad enough that Ski hadn't regained consciousness yet. There were a whole host of problems that could occur with a head injury. Brain swelling and brain damage were a major concern, as was death.

Guilt collided with Kevin's fear. He closed his eyes against the fury that was building and threatened to explode inside him.

Ski was just a kid. Sure, he'd made a few rookie mistakes, but he didn't deserve to die for them. No one did. He was nothing more than an honest officer eager to please those around him. *If he dies, Lord, how am I ever going to bring this news home to Ski's family?*

"I wonder if he even knew what hit him," Jake said, walking back from the ambulance. "Does anyone know where Carlisle is now?"

"I thought you were watching him this afternoon?" Kevin asked.

"I called him in for duty earlier," Jorgensen said. "Then I made a quick call to Carlisle's office just to make sure he was there and was told he'd taken the afternoon off."

"You called?"

With Kevin's surprised expression, Matt shrugged. "It didn't require OT pay."

"We'd only been tailing him to and from his office

and after hours," Jake said. "While he was at the office there wasn't much we could do anyway. Looks like he used that to slip out of view."

Jorgensen propped his hands on his hips. "Well, we have an APB out for him. Maybe we'll get lucky and he won't have left the city."

Jake handed Kevin a pair of boots he'd pulled from the SUV.

"Thanks," Kevin said, immediately sitting on the porch steps to put them on. His feet were freezing, but at least he could feel them. The rest of him had gone numb when he realized Daria wasn't inside.

Officer Johnson emerged from the house. "They found this in the basement. We'll need to dust it for prints."

The officer handed the captain a sealed bag with a tagged item.

Kevin stared into the bag. It was the bloody wrench Daria reported missing during the last break-in.

"You should know that we did get a match from one of the prints we took the other day when the kitchen had been ransacked," Jorgensen said. "They're from a man named Terry Dawson, one of the names on your list from the salvage yard. He's the man who lives a few blocks from here. I wouldn't be surprised at all if that wrench has his prints on it."

"If the prints on the wrench are Terry Dawson's, then that would clear George Carlisle." Anger mixed with mind-numbing fear surged through Kevin at the thought that Carlisle would get away yet again.

"Not necessarily," Jake said. "When I found out Terry Dawson came up as a match, I dug a little deeper into that inch-thick criminal file he has, thinking maybe this would help connect him to Carlisle."

"Did you find anything?" the captain asked.

Jake continued. "No connection yet. Just interesting reading. Dawson is intelligent. A genius, even. Graduated from MIT and was working on his master's until his drug habit got out of control. Since then, his rap sheet tells a pathetic story, but an interesting one.

"Get this. He's an expert in electronics. In fact, it's like his calling card. He's had more misses than hits on conviction even though his rap sheet runs a street block. Why? Because the evidence is always compromised. He used a magnet to erase a video that had him on surveillance robbing a liquor store. He'd set up his contraption the day before. He's calculating and clever, but his drug habit has escalated in the last few years, and sometimes it makes him sloppy."

Kevin took it all in. "Which means he's desperate for money to support that habit."

"Right. But there's more."

"Don't keep me in suspense," Jorgensen said. "Let's have it."

"I did a check on his work record. He was working at the salvage yard just hours before we set up the sting with Carlisle that first night."

"And an electronics expert would know how to create interference for a recording device," Kevin said.

Jorgensen nodded. "Which means Dawson may have been doing Carlisle's dirty work right from the beginning."

Kevin stood up, his mind taking him back to an earlier conversation with Daria. "Carlisle got into trouble with a loan shark some time ago. Daria said he told her that if he didn't pay up he'd be crushed like a tin can."

"The salvage yard crushes old cars before the metal

is sent off to another location for recycling. Do you suppose he took Daria there?" Jake said.

"I'm not waiting to find out." With that, Kevin ran to his SUV, with Jake running right along with him. Behind them, the captain called out, "You call for backup if there's anything. Don't take Carlisle or Dawson by yourselves."

Kevin didn't reply. If he found Daria at the salvage yard with Carlisle, Kevin had no intention of waiting for backup. George Carlisle was going down.

Daria's eyes drifted open to the sound of grinding metal against metal. Then they immediately closed. She was freezing without a jacket on. Her head felt like a watermelon that had just been cracked open and drained. The rocking motion of wherever she was had her stomach doing a somersault. Bile rose up her throat, scorching it. What had George done to her?

She pulled at her hand in an effort to rub the throbbing in her temples and found that she could not move her arms at all. She yanked again, felt pain in her wrists. It took a few seconds to realize her wrists had been bound with rope. She swallowed to help with the cotton-dry taste in her mouth, but it was no use.

She forced her eyes open again. Everything was blurry and refused to come into view. It was almost surreal. Nothing made any sense.

With great effort, Daria tried to lift her head. She had to get out of here, wherever *here* was.

A strange scent permeated the air. She'd smelled it before. Grease and grime. But Daria couldn't place it.

Kevin. Where was he? Would he ever find her? A sob bubbled up her throat, choking her, as it dawned on her that she might never see him again. She'd never had the chance to tell him she loved him. And she did. She loved Kevin with all her heart.

Lord, I know it has taken me a long time to find You. I have Kevin to thank for that. I don't know what to say in prayer. Only that I'm scared and I need Your guidance in any way that can help me or Kevin fight against George.

The words flowed through her mind easily. After a few seconds Daria realized she'd been speaking aloud.

"I don't know if You can hear me, Lord," she said. "Please tell me what to do."

A bright light passed by an opening in the compartment. It illuminated the space just enough for Daria to make out her surroundings. A large set of steel teeth bent into the opening of what looked like a car door. The noise of the steel teeth against metal jarred her. There was no upholstery, no bench seats or rugs on the floor of what she now realized was the shell of a car.

A feeling of renewed terror consumed her. Gears switched and groaned, shrieks of metal cried out as the crane lifted the skeleton of the car in the air. Then, as quickly as it started, it stopped and she was left with only the sound of her pounding heart.

For a moment, Daria felt as light as a feather, floating down in a free fall until the hard, cold metal beneath her slammed into the earth below. Her head bounced up and then snapped back, bringing bright white spots in front of her eyes along with a sharp pain. And then her world went black again.

FIFTEEN

It was a hunch. But it was worth pursuing if it could save someone's life—save *Daria's* life.

"We weren't sloppy that night, Kev," Jake said as he rode in the front seat of the SUV, blue lights flashing on the side streets as they made their way to the salvage yard. "There's no way we could have known Dawson was involved."

"Yeah, we did it right," he said, yet knowing that brought little relief. "We just weren't as cunning as Carlisle and his buddy."

"If Carlisle knew we were there, why would he go to all that trouble? Why not just have Dawson kill Daria right from the start while we were busy with him?"

He cast Jake a hard look, squashing down the image that immediately came to mind. Thank God he hadn't done that. But Jake was right. There were too many questions about Carlisle and his motives.

"Carlisle is sick. He's playing with us."

"What reason would he have for risking it?" Jake asked.

"As long as I find Daria alive, I don't care. Either way, I'm nailing Carlisle to the wall for taking her."

He eased on the brakes as he took the corner too

fast, bending the SUV sharply to one side. Jake held on to the dash.

The lights blazed on the top of the car and the siren screamed. Kevin wanted to warn people he was a man on a mission, desperate to find his woman. And he wanted Carlisle, Dawson and whoever else might be involved to hear him. He wanted them to know he was coming after them.

The dog was going to be a problem, Kevin thought as they broke the lock on the gate.

"Where's Cujo?" Jake asked, glancing around for their unwanted Doberman friend.

Kevin looked around, didn't see the dog anywhere. But he could hear him. "It sounds like he might be locked up inside an office. His bark is too muffled. Keep alert. If Dawson and Carlisle are here, they'll probably spring him on us."

"Wish I'd thought to bring a T-bone steak. Isn't that the way it's done in the movies?"

It was a simple way of breaking the mounting tension, Kevin knew. Easy banter was sometimes the only way to get through a tense shift. Some called it sick, the kinds of jokes cops made about the things they'd seen. Others called it survival. Right now Kevin just wanted to survive the night so he could take Daria home. He so desperately wanted to know they still had a chance at a future together.

Aside from the muffled barking, the salvage yard was eerily quiet as Kevin and Jake moved though the darkness, drawing on shadows and bearing their eyes down on nothing.

"What makes you think they're here?" Jake finally asked.

"It just seems to fit. Dawson works here. Carlisle set up the meeting here. Daria mentioned something about George the day we'd met like I said earlier. And I know Carlisle is a twisted man, very into power games. This seems like the sort of thing that would appeal to him."

On the far side of the lot stood a crane with an arm that jutted out into the sky. Stacked in rows directly next to it were metal blocks that were once cars. Now they looked more like huge cardboard boxes that had been compacted together.

"They're here," Kevin said.

And just as if he could sniff them out, Kevin could hear it. Voices were raised in the corner of the lot. As they moved closer, the voices and the sound of the Doberman's bark grew louder. The dog was definitely inside.

He glanced at Jake, just a quick look that signaled their next move. They slipped into the shadows, listening for the sudden release of the dog, as they crept closer to the building.

Anger surged through Kevin as he approached the two men standing in front of the office door. His gun was snug against his palm, his feet firmly planted on the ground. He and Jake moved into position. The voices grew louder.

Kevin's eyes had acclimated to the darkness enough to distinguish between the two men. George Carlisle stood with his back to them, dressed as if he'd just gone out to an expensive restaurant for dinner. The other man must have been Terry Dawson. He stood sideways facing the yard, dressed in greasy overalls, his hair mussed as if he hadn't showered in days.

"I just want it done and over with. I can't take any more of this," Carlisle said. "Brickster is on my back and that's your fault. If Daria had left town like I planned, you would have been able to get the job done in another city and I'd have my money."

"I told you. If you want me to kill her here, you have to pay me more," Dawson said. "You know the first person they're going to look at is me if they find your ex-wife's body here. I want half the money so I can split."

"Half of nothing is nothing if we both get caught. Just get it over with and then find a way for them to find her body later, somewhere else. You've got connections. Now use them."

"Brickster's the one with connections. He'll use them if it means finally getting his money. But it'll cost you."

Carlisle sneered at Dawson. "Just get the job done."

Jake moved slowly in the other direction to circle around to the other side, careful not to let Carlisle spot him.

"These things can't be rushed," Dawson said. "If this comes back to me—"

"If you do your job right, it won't. Now, if you want your two hundred and fifty thousand dollars, you need to get to work. That bag of crack you have isn't going to last you very long, now, is it?"

"Two hundred and fifty thousand dollars. You'd better not screw me."

Carlisle made a motion as if he was flicking a fly off his shoulder. "I'm in as deep as you are. Now get it done or neither of us gets paid."

Kevin inched closer, still in the shadows, mindful of the noises around him. The grit of dirt under the soles of his boots, the sound of a car in the intersection down the street peeling out as the light changed from red to green.

He squeezed behind a Dumpster. When he emerged

on the other side, Dawson had disappeared and Jake was gone.

Carlisle stood on the grease-stained tar in his Bruno Magli shoes and neatly pressed pants. His leather-gloved fists were planted at his sides and his body was rigid.

By the sound of the argument, Carlisle had been too preoccupied to hear Kevin's approach. Quickly and stealthily, he moved in behind Carlisle and shoved the barrel of the gun against the back of his neck.

Through clenched teeth, Kevin growled. "What have you done with her?"

George started to laugh. "Bang, bang, I guess I'm dead."

"No, you're very much alive, I'm happy to see. But you're going to wish you were dead if you hurt Daria."

"What makes you so sure I hurt Daria at all?"

"Where is she?"

"I don't know what you're talking about."

In one quick move, George twisted around, pulling a gun from the pocket of his jacket as he moved. Keeping a close watch on the gun, Kevin grabbed Carlisle's wrist, but didn't miss George's other fist as it connected with his jaw.

The blow was softened by the gloves George was wearing, but Kevin was momentarily stunned by the impact. He struck back with the butt of his gun, hitting Carlisle square in the nose. Holding tight to George's hand, he twisted the man's arm behind his back until Carlisle was hunched over, staring at the dirt.

"On the ground," he hollered, pushing George and his pristine suit down. He removed the gun, kicking it away from them before handcuffing George.

George spat out blood and then rolled halfway over, glancing up at Kevin.

Kevin shoved the gun in George's face. "Where is she?"

"My, my. Does Daria know about this mean streak of yours?" he taunted.

"You're going to rot in jail, Carlisle."

"If I am, then just know that Daria will be rotting, too. But she'll be in the ground and I'll collect my one million dollars in life insurance."

"Insurance money? That's what this is about?" Kevin reeled for a moment under the impact of this new information, but soon pulled himself together. "How do you suppose you're going to manage that? Insurance companies don't pay out for murders."

"You see, I have that covered. Dawson here thinks he's getting a cut. But he's the one who's going to jail. He's the criminal. I've set it up so that it looks as if he's been blackmailing me for drug money. And when I refused to pay him anymore, he killed Daria in desperation."

"You're finished, Carlisle. You're going down with Dawson whether you like it or not."

George's smile was vile. "You played the game well, Gordon. I just didn't expect that you'd be so moral and watch over Daria yourself. You see, you were just a pawn. Dawson was always going to be the one to kill Daria. But I needed to cast doubt first. I needed the police to harass me enough to watch my every move. You were going to be my alibi while Daria left town and Dawson killed her somewhere else. Sure, I'd be a suspect. The husband always is. But the evidence would show that I was only an innocent bystander in an extortion scheme Dawson set up to get drug money from me."

Realization of the part he'd played in George's plan burned in his gut. "Daria didn't leave town."

"I didn't expect her to be so attached to that dump she lives in. Or to you. But I did count on Dawson being stupid. He thinks he's getting paid." Carlisle chuckled, a trickle of blood spilling out of his mouth where Kevin had hit him. "For all his brains, he'll take the fall. Daria will be dead. And I'll get my money. The public will be outraged that you allowed Daria to die on your watch.

"You know, it would have been a whole lot easier if you'd just let her leave. I knew she was going to want to stay in her house. But sooner or later she would have gotten scared and left on her own. By that time, my story would have been cemented. The police department would have been suspect for harassment. You would have Dawson's prints on file. But you wouldn't leave her alone. So you see, it's your fault she is where she is right now."

"Tell me where she is or—"

"You'll pull the trigger? No, you won't. You're too moral a cop for that."

They were wasting precious time. Jake must have called for backup, because Kevin could hear the sirens in the distance coming closer.

A cruel smile crept up Carlisle's face. "Wonderful. The cavalry is on the way. Go ahead and arrest me. I have set it all up beautifully. I have proof that Dawson was extorting money from me. Your bank records will show that you hired police officers to watch me and Daria. You would never lie about seeing me in the parking lot while Daria's house was being broken into. A jury will believe that the only reason I am here right now is to *save* Daria when I found out that Dawson was trying to kill her.

"You see, I have a letter that poor Dawson wrote to me upon my request while he was…under the influence.

It states his intentions to kill Daria if I don't pay him a certain amount of cash." Carlisle laughed. "The poor fool doesn't even remember writing it. But with that evidence, coupled with police-department harassment, my lawyer will have no trouble getting me out of jail inside of an hour. You'll be investigated for your actions by Internal Affairs and you still won't have your precious Daria. When it all blows over, me and my money will be gone. I call that sweet justice."

Kevin grabbed him by the collar, lifted him off the ground and slammed him back to the dirt again. "Tell me where she is!"

"You're just going to have to find her. But I warn you, it won't be pretty."

Realization slammed hard into him as he heard the roar of a tractor in the far corner of the salvage yard. He stared down at Carlisle. The maniac's eyes were bright and glowing. Kevin glanced over his shoulder to where George was looking. It was hard to see in the dark, but he managed to make out the outline of a compact car being suspended in the air by the arm of a crane.

"Bye, bye, my sweet little Daria," George muttered, before blowing a kiss to the wind.

Kevin's grip loosened and George dropped to the ground like a log.

He swung around and watched the car dangling from the cable, swinging back and forth in the air. He knew the destination was the steel walls of the car crusher. "Please, God, no!" he screamed. "No!"

The ropes were loosening. Daria's jaw hurt from her teeth chattering, from the cold and from shock due to the blow to her head. The burning dread that had started out small in the pit of her stomach grew until it seemed to suck the air right from her lungs. She was going to die. She didn't have a clue where she was or what the engine noises directly outside the stripped-down vehicle were, but it didn't take a genius to know the odds were not good.

The nausea that had enveloped her when she first woke up had subsided. Daria inched her body forward, pushing at the opposite side of the car to get closer to give herself leverage to lift up. She had to think fast. She had to move. She couldn't die here in this car and not at least give it every ounce of energy she had to survive.

She was just about able to rise onto her elbow when a screeching noise, followed by a bang on the roof of the car, startled her. As the car was lifted into the air, she lost her balance and smacked her head against the steel floor beneath her. Her cheek slammed against the metal and exploded with pain.

She closed her eyes and thought back to a prayer she'd heard in church. *For Thou wilt light my candle: the Lord my God will enlighten my darkness.*

If it was God's will, Daria knew she would die. But not without every bit of fight she had left inside her.

Kevin couldn't see who was running the crane, but he had a good idea it was Dawson. The guy's mind was about as twisted as the metal parts strewn about the salvage yard. Terror ripped through him thinking about what Daria had already been through.

She was probably lying helpless in one of these cars ready to be crushed. He prayed she was still alive and that he would get to her in time.

The words echoed in his head like a throbbing headache that wouldn't go away. Kevin couldn't stand to think of Daria dying that way. *Please, Lord, if she has to die, don't make her suffer that fate.*

As he sprinted, dodging piles of scrap metal and cubes that used to be cars, he gauged the distance between the crane and car crusher and knew he would have to either be superhuman or granted a miracle from God to make it in time.

Blood pumped through his veins as he saw the car lifting into the air, saw the sneer in Dawson's eyes as he ground gears to move the mammoth arm of the crane to position the car above the crusher.

Kevin ran, his eyes darting from the vehicle, to the man in the seat of the crane, to the ground he had left to cross. He wasn't going to make it. The magnet holding the car released and the compact dropped into place between the thick walls of steel. His lungs burned, his chest pounded. Daria. His sweet, stubborn, wonderful Daria.

"No!" he screamed from somewhere that sounded outside his body. A shot rang out and then another just as the walls slammed in around the car. "Daria!"

Jake appeared, pushing a limp Dawson out of the driver's seat. He took the controls of the crusher, but it was already too late. Metal squealed as it compacted into an object nearly one-third the size of its original form.

There was another scream, harsh and loud and deafening that came from Kevin's body. He felt the horror of what he'd just seen rip itself from his lungs and explode into the night as he fell to his knees.

"Oh, God," he cried. "No, please, God. This isn't happening."

Kevin was vaguely aware of the sound of feet hitting the ground around him as he stared at the mangled metal, listening to the faraway sounds of sirens and tires screeching to a halt. Somehow, after all the noise and destruction, the world had gotten eerily quiet except in his head. The noise there was too unbearable.

Kevin climbed to his feet and pushed forward, but was held back by force.

"No. Don't do it," Jake said. "You can't do this to yourself."

"I've got to help her," Kevin cried. "She's in there. Get out of my way."

"She's gone, Kev. If she was in that car, there is no way she could have possibly survived."

"No, I have to get to her. What are you doing?" Kevin pushed against Jake until he stumbled. But his partner held on tight.

"I'm not letting you do this," he said.

Tears streamed down Kevin's cheeks, making it impossible to see Jake. But he heard the anguish in his partner's voice and knew his words were true. Daria was gone. Unable to stand it, he collapsed back to the ground.

His whole body went numb and his arms felt so achingly empty.

He swallowed a sob, but it managed to break free. "I love her." He loved Daria and now she was gone.

Swarms of police officers scurried around them, but Kevin didn't care. He'd failed and lost the one person who'd meant the world to him.

Carlisle was on his feet, being ushered into the back of a police car. From somewhere near the crane, Kevin heard another officer shout that Dawson was dead of a gunshot wound. The cavalry *had* arrived. But it was too late to save his Daria.

* * *

Daria couldn't think beyond the pain in her body. Her wrists ached from pulling at the ropes for so long. But when they'd finally slipped from her hands, she'd been able to open the car door enough to get out.

The fall from the car hadn't seemed all that long until she was actually airborne. But what choice had she really had when looking back at the compacted steel blocks around her, knowing she was startlingly close to being crushed inside one of them?

She must have blacked out for a moment upon impact with the ground. She didn't know for how long. All she knew now was that her face hurt as well as her shoulder and hips. Her body screamed at her to the point that she really didn't want to open her eyes and move for the next hundred years. The cold from the snowbank she'd fallen into made her body shiver violently. But if not for the snow, the fall might have killed her.

Kevin's tormented voice pealed into the dark night. "God, please! No."

Relief washed over her and she could hardly hold back the choking sob that was lodged in her throat. She had to get to Kevin. But with each attempt to roll over, pain shot through her body.

"Kevin!" she called out weakly, wondering if he could hear her over all the commotion. The night sky flashed with blue-and-white lights, but inside her little corner of the yard, she lay undisturbed.

The soul-gutting sobs from Kevin broke her heart and had her wanting to cry out to him to tell him, no, she was not dead. But she couldn't form the words. "I'm here," she called in a weak voice.

A beam of light swept over her as she rolled to her side.

"I found her!" the officer yelled.

Within seconds, a flurry of activity overwhelmed her. It was Kevin's face she searched for and finally saw come into view before she slipped into darkness.

Thank You, Lord, was the only thing on Kevin's mind as he held Daria. He couldn't ever remember going from such utter terror to such complete joy in the span of seconds. He thought he'd lost Daria forever. And the thought of that had leveled him.

But his sweet Daria wasn't dead at all. She was here and she was very much alive in his arms. His tears of rage transformed to tears of joy as he knelt beside her.

Jake was behind him. "The ambulance is on the way. Is she okay?"

"I don't know," Kevin said, carefully brushing the dirt from her face, afraid to touch her and wanting to blanket her in his arms. "She's freezing. I need a blanket. But she's alive. For now, that's all that matters."

Looking over his shoulder at the arm of the crane, Jake said, "Man, that fall alone could have killed her. It's a good thing we had all this snow to cushion her fall."

Kevin leaned down and brushed his lips against Daria's scraped forehead in an effort to shut out the images colliding in his brain of what might have been. He only wanted to feel the relief that this nightmare would soon be over.

He rode with her in the ambulance to the hospital. She'd gone in and out of consciousness, calling his name.

"I'm right here," he said.

"Thank You, God," she whispered, drifting in and out of the haze.

* * *

She was going to be okay, the doctor had told Kevin after the initial examination. With those few tiny words, relief shot through him, quick and strong.

"Is she conscious? I need to see her," Kevin said.

"Like I told your captain, she's not ready to answer questions about what happened. If this can wait at all, I'd prefer you come back in the morning after she's had a chance to sleep and get some of the fogginess out of her head."

No, it definitely could not wait. He had to see with his own eyes that she was alive and was going to stay that way for a very long time. Kevin needed to hold Daria in his arms or else he was going to go mad.

"I won't be long."

The doctor sighed. "Only for a few minutes."

This wasn't police business. Kevin didn't want to ask Daria anything more than for her to never leave him like that again. Ever.

He had realized pretty fast tonight that he was desperately in love with the woman. If he didn't know it before, he knew it the moment he thought he'd lost her forever. God had answered his prayers in giving Daria the strength to get out of that car before it was crushed.

He pushed through the hospital-room door and found Daria lying on the bed and he knew the nightmare was really over. They could move beyond this and be just the two of them.

"How do you feel?" he said, pushing back the stray strand of hair that had fallen in her face.

"Sore. Those meds haven't quite taken effect yet."

"They will soon. No more pain, I promise." And no more fear. He'd make sure of that.

She shook her head. "George is in jail now?"

"Yes. And he's staying there. I've already spoken to the D.A. and Martha said with your testimonial and all the other evidence George thought he could use to prove his innocence, she's sure she can get a conviction. If you hadn't survived, he might have gotten away with it."

"I didn't know what to do when I saw him at the house. It all happened so fast."

"If he hadn't been there with Dawson, it would have been harder to prove they were working together. But your testimony and Ski's will seal it."

"Ski? I almost forgot. Is he…?"

"They weren't sure at first, but he's going to be fine. They took him into surgery to relieve the pressure on his brain from the blow to his head. But the doctor feels they got to him in time."

"And the other man?"

"Terry Dawson? He's dead. He was the one who'd been vandalizing your house. Not the kids in the neighborhood."

"It's a nice neighborhood then."

"A great neighborhood to raise a family."

Daria smiled, leaning her head against the pillow. "You know, the whole time I was in that car I kept thanking God that He brought you into my life. And I prayed that He'd give me the chance to see you again."

"Then He answered both of our prayers." Kevin kissed Daria's hand. "I want you with me for the rest of my life, Daria. I want to marry you."

A tear trickled down her cheek. "Nothing would make me happier. Even if I have to take Dramamine every day while we sail around the world."

Kevin laughed and reached forward, kissing Daria on

the lips. "Well, maybe not 'around' the world. But a sail down the coast for our honeymoon might be nice."

Daria sighed and closed her eyes, moving her head restlessly from side to side on the pillow. The meds were taking hold. Soon, she'd be asleep. And when she woke this time, she wouldn't wake to her nightmare.

"Are you going to be here when I wake up?" she asked quietly.

"I'll stay as long as you need me to."

"I think I finally understand why my mother packed her bags and moved around the country with my father. When I was a kid, I thought it was so crazy. But Dad was her home. As long as they were together she had a home. She loved him as much as I love you."

"I like hearing you say that."

"I like saying it."

"I love you, too," he said softly in her ear. And then he kissed her and gazed into her eyes.

The smile that filled her eyes said it all. She was home.

* * * * *

Dear Reader,

Writing *Yuletide Protector* was exciting as well as challenging. My husband is a police officer and while he's incredibly supportive of my writing, he doesn't read my books. This was the first book that he and I really had a chance to work on together while I researched Kevin Gordon's character. As I wrote the story, I'd come to a part where I needed police information and all I had to do was walk into the next room and he was there to have an hour-long discussion with me about what I was trying to do and whether it would work. I hope there are many more books we can work on together like that.

This book was a surprising challenge for me though. Most of the stories I write feature characters who have either strong faith, have lost faith or have drifted away from their relationship with God. I've never written a story about someone who had no relationship at all, good or bad, with the Lord.

I hemmed and hawed and struggled as I wrote Daria Carlisle's story as she fell in love with her protector, Kevin Gordon, a devoted Christian who couldn't allow himself to fall in love with a woman unless she shared his Christian faith. I'll even admit I complained about my plight to my dear friend and fellow Love Inspired author Pamela Tracy, who in her wisdom told me to accept the challenge and that it'll probably be the best book I've ever written.

Well, I'll leave that to you readers to decide. But I will say that despite the challenge, writing this book required me to dig deeper into my own feelings about faith, solidifying for me why I'm a Christian. And for that I'll always be happy that I wrote Daria Carlisle's story. I hope you enjoy it, too.

I love hearing from readers. Please check out the CRAFTIE Ladies of Suspense blog at http://www.ladiesofsuspense.blogspot.com or write me at LisaMondello@aol.com.

Many blessings,

Lisa Mondello

QUESTIONS FOR DISCUSSION

1. Sometimes there is a fine line between guiding and pushing someone. In *Yuletide Protector,* Kevin needs to walk that line. What does he do to help guide Daria in her faith journey without pushing her?

2. At first, Daria doesn't believe that her ex-husband would hurt her, even after Kevin explained what he'd done. Have you ever known someone or known of someone who thought a person was harmless only to find out later that they were wrong?

3. Daria feels very alone and thinks that owning her house will make her feel grounded. Have you ever felt you had no one to turn to? How did you deal with it?

4. Daria had never known God in her life before she met Kevin. How did she come to know Christ and accept Him in her heart?

5. Kevin feels responsible for the fact that Daria's ex-husband is not in jail. Do you think his feelings are justified?

6. Daria feels a strong attachment to the house she's renovating. How do her feelings change as the story progresses? What does she learn about "home"?

7. Daria confesses to Kevin that she doesn't know any prayers and he tells her that prayer is just a con-

versation with the Lord. What are your feelings about prayer?

8. Many people move throughout their lives, such as people in the military. How did moving so much affect Daria and her relationship with others?

9. Kevin and his family experienced tragedy when he was young. How did that affect him and his decision to be a police officer?

10. Kevin is so focused on George Carlisle's quest to murder his ex-wife that he misses the fact that he was being used. Could he have seen this coming and done something differently?

11. In church communities it's common to see neighbors reaching out to neighbors. What was different about Kevin's approach to Daria's neighbors than her own? Do you think it was a reflection of their personalities, their upbringings or part of his faith?

12. Have you ever known someone who has taken the same faith journey as Daria, going from being a nonbeliever to accepting Christ in their lives? How did this affect you?

Here is an exciting sneak preview of
TWIN TARGETS by Marta Perry,
the first book in the new 6-book
Love Inspired Suspense series
PROTECTING THE WITNESSES
available beginning January 2010.

Deputy U.S. Marshal Micah McGraw forced down the sick feeling in his gut. A law enforcement professional couldn't get emotional about crime victims. He could imagine his police chief father saying the words. Or his FBI agent big brother. They wouldn't let emotion interfere with doing the job.

"Pity." The local police chief grunted.

Natural enough. The chief hadn't known Ruby Maxwell, aka Ruby Summers. He hadn't been the agent charged with relocating her to this supposedly safe environment in a small village in Montana. He didn't have to feel responsible for her death.

"This looks like a professional hit," Chief Burrows said.

"Yeah."

He knew only too well what was in the man's mind. What would a professional hit man be doing in the remote reaches of western Montana? Why would anyone want to kill this seemingly inoffensive waitress?

And most of all, what did the U.S. Marshals Service have to do with it?

All good questions. Unfortunately he couldn't answer

any of them. Secrecy was the crucial element that made the Federal Witness Protection Service so successful. Breach that, and everything that had been gained in the battle against organized crime would be lost.

His cell buzzed and he turned away to answer it. "McGraw."

"You wanted the address for the woman's next of kin?" asked one of his investigators.

"Right." Ruby had a twin sister, he knew. She'd have to be notified. Since she lived back east, at least he wouldn't be the one to do that.

"Jade Summers. Librarian. Current address is 45 Rock Lane, White Rock, Montana."

For an instant Micah froze. "Are you sure of that?"

"'Course I'm sure."

After he hung up, Micah turned to stare once more at the empty shell that had been Ruby Summers. She'd made mistakes in her life, plenty of them, but she'd done the right thing in the end when she'd testified against the mob. She hadn't deserved to end up lifeless on a cold concrete floor.

As for her sister...

What exactly was an easterner like Jade Summers doing in a small town in Montana? If there was an innocent reason, he couldn't think of it.

Ruby must have tipped her off to her location. That was the only explanation, and the deed violated one of the major principles of witness protection.

Ruby had known the rules. Immediate family could be relocated with her. If they chose not to, no contact was permitted—ever.

Ruby's twin had moved to Montana. White Rock was probably forty miles or so east of Billings. Not exactly around the corner from her sister.

But the fact that she was in Montana had to mean that they'd been in contact. And that contact just might have led to Ruby's death.

He glanced at his watch. Once his team arrived, he'd get back on the road toward Billings and beyond, to White Rock. To find Jade Summers and get some answers.

* * * * *

Will Micah get to Jade in time to save
her from a similar fate?
Find out in TWIN TARGETS,
available January 2010
from Love Inspired Suspense.

Love Inspired.
HISTORICAL
INSPIRATIONAL HISTORICAL ROMANCE

Drake Amberly, duke of Hawk Haven, came to the colonies for revenge—to unmask the spy who killed his brother. Yet he finds himself distracted from his mission by the beautiful and spirited Elise Cooper. But as Drake's pursuit of the "Fox" brings him dangerously close to Elise's secrets, she must prove to him that love and forgiveness are all they need.

Look for
The Duke's Redemption
by
CARLA CAPSHAW

*Available January
wherever books are sold.*

www.SteepleHill.com

Steeple
Hill®
LIH82828

REQUEST YOUR FREE BOOKS!
2 FREE RIVETING INSPIRATIONAL NOVELS
PLUS 2 FREE MYSTERY GIFTS

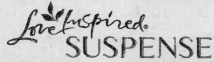

YES! Please send me 2 FREE Love Inspired® Suspense novels and my 2 FREE mystery gifts (gifts are worth about $10). After receiving them, if I don't wish to receive any more books, I can return the shipping statement marked "cancel". If I don't cancel, I will receive 4 brand-new novels every month and be billed just $4.24 per book in the U.S. or $4.74 per book in Canada. That's a savings of over 20% off the cover price. It's quite a bargain! Shipping and handling is just 50¢ per book.* I understand that accepting the 2 free books and gifts places me under no obligation to buy anything. I can always return a shipment and cancel at any time. Even if I never buy another book, the two free books and gifts are mine to keep forever.

123 IDN EYM2 323 IDN EYNE

Name	(PLEASE PRINT)	
Address		Apt. #
City	State/Prov.	Zip/Postal Code

Signature (if under 18, a parent or guardian must sign)

Mail to Steeple Hill Reader Service:
IN U.S.A.: P.O. Box 1867, Buffalo, NY 14240-1867
IN CANADA: P.O. Box 609, Fort Erie, Ontario L2A 5X3

Not valid to current subscribers of Love Inspired Suspense books.

Want to try two free books from another series?
Call 1-800-873-8635 or visit www.morefreebooks.com

* Terms and prices subject to change without notice. Prices do not include applicable taxes. Sales tax applicable in N.Y. Canadian residents will be charged applicable provincial taxes and GST. Offer not valid in Quebec. This offer is limited to one order per household. All orders subject to approval. Credit or debit balances in a customer's account(s) may be offset by any other outstanding balance owed by or to the customer. Please allow 4 to 6 weeks for delivery. Offer available while quantities last.

Your Privacy: Steeple Hill Books is committed to protecting your privacy. Our Privacy Policy is available online at www.SteepleHill.com or upon request from the Reader Service. From time to time we make our lists of customers available to reputable third parties who may have a product or service of interest to you. If you would prefer we not share your name and address, please check here. ☐

TITLES AVAILABLE NEXT MONTH

Available December 29, 2009

FINDING HER WAY HOME by Linda Goodnight
Redemption River

She came to Oklahoma to escape her past, but single dad
Trace Bowman isn't about to let Cheyenne Rhodes hide her
heart away. But will he stand by her when he learns the secret
she's running from?

THE DOCTOR'S PERFECT MATCH by Irene Hannon
Lighthouse Lane

Dr. Christopher Morgan is *not* looking for love. Especially with
Marci Clay. The physician and the waitress come from two very
different worlds. Worlds that are about to collide in faith and love.

HER FOREVER COWBOY by Debra Clopton
Men of Mule Hollow

Mule Hollow, Texas, is chock-full of handsome cowboys. Veterinarian
Susan Worth moves in, dreaming of meeting Mr. Right, who most
certainly is *not* the gorgeous rescue worker blazing through town...or
is he?

THE FAMILY NEXT DOOR by Barbara McMahon

Widower Joe Kincaid doesn't want his daughter liking their pretty
new neighbor. His little girl's lost too much already. And he doesn't
think the city girl will last a month in their small Maine town. But
Gillian Parker isn't what he expected.

A SOLDIER'S DEVOTION by Cheryl Wyatt
Wings of Refuge

Pararescue jumper Vince Reardon doesn't want to accept
Valentina Russo's heartfelt apologies for wrecking his motorcycle....
Until she shows this soldier what true devotion is really about.

MENDING FENCES by Jenna Mindel

Called home to care for her ailing mother, Laura Toivo finds herself in
uncertain territory. With the help of neighbor Jack Stahl, she'll learn
that life is all about connections, and that love is the greatest gift.

LICNMBPA1209